Forever Summer

by

Nicole Bea

Forever Summer

COPYRIGHT © 2020 by Nicole Bea

Cover Art by *Diana Carlile*

The Wild Rose Press, Inc.
PO Box 708
Adams Basin, NY 14410-0708
Visit us at www.thewildrosepress.com

Publishing History
First Young Adult Edition, 2020
Print ISBN 978-1-5092-3020-4
Digital ISBN 978-1-5092-3021-1

Published in the United States of America

"We could have texted if you wanted to talk," I remind him, patting the spot on the bed where my phone has slipped down to.

He pulls an elastic band from his wrist and snaps it into place around his hair, making a perfectly small bun before taking the towel, squeezing the excess water from the style, and taking a seat at the edge of my bed. "You're trying to make it sound like you don't want me here, but I know you do. You wouldn't have let me in otherwise, and you wouldn't have kissed me this afternoon." There's a pause, the night dripping in and our faces drawing closer. "Do you believe in love at first sight, Morrigan?" His voice hangs heavy and warm in the bedroom air.

The question might be a rhetorical one, but I feel compelled to answer because I think I gave a shit answer the first time he asked me the question.

"I used to," I reply softly, a whispered lilt to my voice that matches his own. "You know, before." I tuck a loose strand of hair behind my ear.

"That's interesting." He clasps his hands together and rests them between his thighs. His eyes tell me that isn't the answer he wanted. "You stopped believing in love at first sight when I finally started."

Dedication

To forever summers, wild hearts, and love at first sight.
May they be everything you've ever dreamed of.

Chapter 1

Both my mind and body are restless—a leg-shaking, hangnail-picking, sighing-impatiently restless that only comes with being stuck somewhere I don't want to be for a long period of time. My phone has already blinked off in the middle of my favorite song, a big, red, battery-depleted symbol flashing on the screen. Now I'm stuck on this plane with nothing to do but wait. I don't bother taking my headphones off because I prefer the conversations around me to be muffled, people making small talk with their neighbors, reading pamphlets, or day-drinking the flight away. They're all restless too, waiting to get to Birmingham.

On top of it all, I hate the idea of being what feels like a million feet in the air, but on the afternoon following the embarrassingly small Independence Day parade in Bear Point, Michigan, that's where I find myself. The stewardess on the Boeing 737—or 747 or some combination of numbers that mean nothing to me—tells us to secure our seatbelts while we prepare for some turbulence. The craft dips, making me claw at the shared armrest of my chair, only to find the figure next to me has had the exact same idea. To my dismay, our fingers touch, and she looks at me with that older lady smile a mother gives a nervous child.

"It's a little windy up here today," the dark-haired woman says as if I didn't already notice.

1

I'm not awake enough to deal with her small talk. Instead, I force a tight-lipped grin to placate her before placing my head back against the seat with my eyes closed. Maybe if I fall back asleep, I'll come around just in time for us to land in Alabama, and then I can figure out how I'm going to survive the summer on a ranch I don't want to be at.

The idea of seeing my father again makes me a little bit nervous, forcing me to adjust the leather bracelet around my wrist. I haven't seen him in at least four years now, which doesn't sound like a lot, but so much has happened in those four years.

I could start with twelve and a half weeks ago when my boyfriend cracked my eye socket with his fist after I broke up with him, and then I could end somewhere around the time I was found in the bathroom in a tub filled with my own blood, but those events pale in comparison to all the things that lie between. It's been a rough four years since my father left, and an even worse twelve and a half weeks since Fitz and I were separated. Based on all the conversations I overheard behind closed doors, my mother needs the break from me and the scars hidden under my bracelet just as much as I need the break from Michigan.

"Hi, folks." A man's crisp voice crackles over the overhead speaker of the airplane, the pilot, presumably. "We are nearing our destination in Birmingham and are going to begin our descent. Please return to your seats and ensure your seat belts are fastened for the duration of the trip. Thank you for flying with us today, and we hope you had a pleasant journey."

People adjusting their positions create a shuffle—

tray tables up, seat backs forward—and I adjust my own chair so I am sitting straight up instead of slightly reclined.

"So where are you headed?" the lady asks, clearly not taking my silence for the brush-off it was intended to be. "Visiting a boyfriend?"

She gives me a kooky smile, and I recoil at the word. *Boyfriend*. My hand instinctively reaches for the spot under my eye, an area where the swelling has gone down and returned to normal color.

"I'm going to see my father, actually," I reply point-blank, shuffling the back of my pixie cut. "I haven't seen him in a long time."

"Oh, well, that's nice." She doesn't seem to be listening to the undertones of the answer. "I'm going to see my new grandbaby, Max." She's effectively talking to herself at this point but doesn't seem to mind. "He's just the cutest. Started talking the other week." The woman laughs a little bit too loudly, and I shrink down in my seat so nobody can see me. "So your father, huh? That's got to be exciting. Good for you."

Thankfully, she pulls out a phone from her purse and starts shuffling through it, as if she suddenly realizes she doesn't want to talk to me just as much as I don't really want to converse with her. I'm just about to close my eyes again when she leans over to show me a photograph of a fat child in a onesie.

"This is Max!" she announces with a proud tone. "Isn't he just the most precious thing? Debbie wanted to call him Isaiah after the Lord's book, but then once he was born, Max just stuck like glue!"

The bumbling baby in the picture has the palest skin I've ever seen, with a huge spit bubble falling out of his mouth and a handful of soft cheezies. I'm not sure what's so precious about that; the combination of saliva and powdered orange slime kind of makes me nauseous.

We hit another bump, and it dawns on me that we've finally landed and I can get out of this chair and away from Chatty Cathy. However, the alternative doesn't seem to have many additional benefits. I'll have to have an awkward conversation with my father all the way to the ranch. Maybe I can get away with not telling him my entire life story because my mother has likely relayed all of the required information to him anyway.

They still talk so much. It's weird. I thought when people got a divorce it was because they hated the other person, but it seems like perhaps, in this case, something fell apart other than the whole love aspect. I don't think it was anything like what drove me and Fitz apart—my mother wouldn't send me to Alabama if it was—but still I almost want to get to the point where I can ask the question without seeming like a nosy child just trying to get all up in her parents' business.

"We have now landed in Birmingham, Alabama. Local time is 1:17 p.m. Thank you for flying American Airlines and have a lovely stay, a relaxing stopover, or a beautiful vacation."

I snort at the last part of the pilot's final message. I can't imagine anyone coming to Alabama for a vacation, let alone a beautiful one.

Twenty-five minutes later I'm dragging my big, red suitcase across the atrium of the Birmingham Airport, the wheels clacking on the tile floor. My phone is in my other hand, but the battery is dead, and I'm a little bit lost without the device to look at as I walk through crowds of people while trying to find the exit of this damn place. Just as I think I've found my way to the outside world, a familiar voice calls my name toward the blaring exit sign.

"Morrigan!"

Whipping around, I come face-to-face with my father. He almost looks like a stranger with his close-cropped hair and bushy beard, a cowboy hat in one hand as he pulls me in to give me an obligatory hug. My hands are full of bag handles, my phone, and a hoodie I don't know why I put on for the plane. My contribution to the embrace is standing there and pretending not to feel strange at the idea of being hugged by this man who left Michigan and found his happiness in opening a ranch.

"How was your flight? I like the short hair, kiddo. Suits your face."

If he notices my standoffish nature, he doesn't say anything about it. Maybe he's feeling as awkward about the whole thing as I am, but just has the life experience to know how to hide it better.

"Hi, Dad. It was okay."

"God, you've grown a ton. You look exactly like your mother when I met her. How is she, anyway? I spoke to her on the phone earlier after you left, and she sounded like she missed you already."

Somehow, I doubt that. "She's fine. Don't you talk to her all the time?"

Dad takes my suitcase, and we walk toward the front doors of the airport. There's a black Chevrolet Silverado parked in the waiting lot, and he steers me toward it. "I do, that's true." He laughs, gently tossing my bags into the cab of the truck. With that tiny gesture, suddenly the icy waters between us warm. "I never stopped liking her, Morrigan. She's a good woman."

Normally, I'd say something snide, but the warm Alabama air is doing something to my insides. Instead, I adjust the soft band around my wrist and open the passenger's side door, the handle searing from the hot temperatures. I clamber into the vehicle unceremoniously, used to my mother's Matrix instead of the large pickup, and use a good portion of my strength to slam the door shut. The sound echoes through the silence between my father and me, reverberating off the road noise.

"So are you excited to see the ranch?" Dad turns the key in the ignition, and the engine roars to life. "We've got horses up the ying-yang. I thought maybe this summer we'd teach you how to ride."

The idea of sitting on a horse makes me nervous. "Maybe. I don't know. I'm not really a country person, Dad. This is all a little strange to me. Can't I just plant vegetables or something and say I'm reformed?"

Dad gives me the side-eye, merging onto the highway. "What happened there, anyway?"

"You mean Mom didn't tell you?" I nervously twist the soft strap that covers my scars.

"Oh, she did. I just want to hear the story from you. You know, I tried to come up there after everything happened, but your mother told me just to stay put. She didn't want to stress you out anymore."

"So now she's sent me to you anyway."

"You make this sound like a prison sentence, Mo. Most girls would kill to spend a summer with a herd of horses and a couple of months of sunshine. From what I remember, you used to be one of those girls."

I sigh, staring out the window, suddenly tired. Flatness rolls past, green and red and brown like unseasonal Christmas, American flags flying on posts and the fronts of houses that are few and far between and pushed back well off the main road. The sky is a cerulean blue with a nip of white cotton clouds, all way up high in the atmosphere as if they're wisps that might blow away at any possible second. The land is beautiful and open. Maybe the pilot was onto something after all. Something is redeeming about the flats of Alabama, the rustic nature scene well outside of Birmingham, and the drive toward Colbourn Creek where the ranch was founded. The little girl Dad remembers is gone. Somewhere along the line, the dreams he speaks of turned to nightmares, and the imaginary friends became demons.

The radio croons a song about love or loss or something I only half pick up on, while Dad turns the knob on the stereo, increasing the sound.

"You don't have to tell me about it now, Morrigan. But some point this summer I'd like to know why that shit of a boyfriend of yours isn't in jail."

"Ex-boyfriend," I correct, flatly. Dad ignores my tone, and I ignore his cursing.

"Whichever it is, he hurt you badly. And you hurt yourself badly as a result. Those things don't make a father happy for his daughter. I just want to help you, and I think you'll figure that out as time goes on."

That is what time does, I've learned. It goes on.

By the time I see signs for Colbourn Creek, the song has changed at least another six times. Long, green fields and bushy trees populate the edge of the roadside as we bump off onto a dirt road, little pebbles shooting up from underneath the thick tires of the truck. A half mile down the road, give or take, a sign made of horseshoes reads *Tin Star Ranch* and hangs from between two tall posts erected at the end of the driveway. In the distance, a log house and a large log barn poke their way up into the midday horizon, while spattered along the emerald and dust of the grass are clumps of horses, spotted and speckled and every color I've ever seen a horse be.

It's breathtaking and overwhelming all at once, and the expression on my face must give me away.

"Thoughts?" Dad asks as we rumble up the rickety road, the driveway only adding to the charm of the entire estate. We pull into an empty spot in the front of the house, and I don't answer him. This time it's not by choice. I'm actually speechless because I think a farm like this was my dream when I was a kid.

As I try to put my thoughts together, a figure on a little brown horse rides around the corner. He's tanned with shoulder-length raven hair, maybe nineteen or twenty years old at most, with an equally black cowboy hat perched on his head and a pair of dusty work gloves on his hands. He guides the animal with whispered ease, coming to a stop at my father's side of the truck. The horse gives a little snort as my father opens his door and slides out.

By the time I situate all my belongings into one arm, my dad is at the passenger's side door, opening it and offering me a hand down.

"Levy, this is my daughter, Morrigan. She'll be staying here with us for the summer. I was thinking maybe we'd teach her to ride. She's from Bear Point,

Michigan, just outside the city. This is all kind of a new thing for her."

Levy's dark gaze pierces my own, and he gives me a quick half smile. It's not as if I suddenly forget about Fitz when I look at Levy. In fact, quite the opposite happens. Staring up at the broad man with the fence-built shoulders and summer skin, I realize, although my interest is piqued, my rebounding wall has been erected. Fitz has ruined me for other men, killed my ability to have confidence in my words, and beaten me into a quiet type of submission that I don't know if I'll ever get out of. The only way I can fight is with attitude and self-harm, and neither of those is natural given this situation.

"Morrigan, meet Levy Rider. There's a pun in the name that's more than appropriate as he's my best horse trainer. You'll find him around here on the ranch more days than not. And this little horse here is Rosie. She's an old girl but nice and steady. Good for heading out in the field and checking on the fence lines."

Rosie heaves a great sigh as if she's done more work today than I'll get done all summer, and pokes her nose out toward me. Hesitantly, I reach my hand up and stroke the soft velvet of the white stripe running down her face.

"Michigan, huh?" Levy asks, a bit of an amused and accented lilt to his voice. "We'll turn you into a country girl in no time."

I somehow doubt that, but I'm sure he and my dad will make a valiant effort.

Between the two of them, they don't wait for a response, as if something in my father's posture tells Levy I'm not going to respond. They start talking about ranch business, using terms I've never heard of, speaking a language only they seem to comprehend. Tossing my carry-on bag on the front porch, I make myself scarce, a habit I've picked up over the last few months, feigning interest in the flowers and bushes accenting the house. It's easier to pretend to be interested in things that don't ask me questions or expect my participation. Instead, I touch the soft petals that line the porch steps while I listen in on both my father's questions and the southern accent drowning the answers Levy gives.

"Did the trailer come in today?" my dad asks. "Couple of rescue ponies coming in we could do some work with."

Levy shifts his weight on Rosie's back and puts both reins in the opposite hand. "Tomorrow. Got caught up with a washed-out road and had to turn back to the highway. Gordon's good, though. He'll take care of those horses like they're his own."

Dad nods, looking over at me. "I think one of them might make a good project for Morrigan. We'll see what they're like when we unload in the morning."

My name prickles in my ears. A project horse? I don't know anything about horses, and my comprehensive list of current interests could fit in the palm of my hand: reading Fitz's messages, listening to music, and not being here.

"Sounds good, sir." Levy wipes at the back of his neck. "I'm off to check the north pasture. I'll be about an hour, then I'll come back to prep grain and finish stalls. We've got a trail group coming in at quarter to five, and Declan's going to take the tail end of that."

With a mutual nod between him and my father,

Levy and Rosie trot off down the driveway, little puddles of dust forming by the horse's hooves. I watch Levy's muscles ripple over his shoulders and back, the tight black T-shirt straining at the arm cuffs. He doesn't look like any teenager I've ever seen in Michigan, though for all I know, at this point he could be thirty and married with ten kids, fourteen dogs, a Chevy Tahoe, and a house on the beach.

"Well, what do you think of that?" Dad's voice interrupts my internal dialogue, and it hits me that I've been daydreaming for an awkwardly long time. I nod, not really knowing exactly what he's talking about.

"You know, Mo, there was one point in your life when you would have been so excited to have a horse to yourself for the summer. You begged for riding lessons for ages. I just can't believe how much has changed in four years."

Dad hauls my suitcase out of the cab of the truck and places it down on the gravel drive. I want to tell him there was a time in my life when I would have been excited about a lot of things, but Fitz knocked most of them out of me. I hate that I've let him ruin my life; maybe that's why I tried to end it.

"Sorry." I apologize because I guiltily feel the need to. "I just—I don't know. This is a lot to process. And I kind of have a lot going on already."

Dad tips his cowboy hat to keep the sun from shining directly into his eyes. "I understand that, Mo. But I wish you'd just let me into what exactly is happening from your perspective so I could try and help you."

"Don't really want to talk about it. I know already know, and to me, at this point, that's enough."

11

My father sighs and picks up the dusky red suitcase, heading toward the house as if he's exasperated with me already, and it's only been an hour. I think he expects me to follow, but I don't because I'm a little bit annoyed. I plunk myself on the bumper of the truck, stuck in a driveway alcove, and watch the sun beat down on the field of multi-colored horses. Two of them appear to be playing, nipping at each other's manes and loping off across the parched field. Young colts perhaps, doting on each other with mothers watching closely nearby. A warm wind whistles against the perimeter of the ranch, and I decide to take a walk to explore my temporary home and think about all the ways in which this summer isn't going to fix me from being entirely broken.

Chapter 2

I brush my bangs from my face, hair sticky with heat, and watch as Levy and Rosie disappear over the crest of the north hill. The reality is once I step inside that door, this is all real. I'm really here. I'm trading my traffic-heavy, bustling city home in Michigan for a quiet ranch in Alabama where another car hasn't been seen in miles.

There are fences as far as I can see, tall, wooden, post-and-rail, rustic gates with shiny handles and hinges. White-wrapped marshmallows of hay sit out in the fields in stacks and rows that look like ground-ridden clouds, while cut trails between trees and worn paths around paddocks are filled with grass and weeds trying to grow over ever so slowly. The sun is a lemony yellow up high in the sky, the afternoon burning on and warming the fields and horses and rooftops of the countryside. I walk along the pasture for what must be a half hour, ducking under the boards back and forth, following a family of ducks headed for a center pond to the west. A little Appaloosa pretends not to be watching me, but he is.

"Hey." A voice comes from behind me, the thudding in the grass a familiar sound by now. Still, the sound makes me jump half out of my skin, as I barely heard the horse hooves approaching. Levy must have pulled Rosie up in a slow walk, something to startle me on purpose.

"Jesus Christ! You trying to give me a heart attack?" I whip around and come face-to-nose with Rosie's white muzzle.

Levy chuckles softly, leaning on the horn of the saddle. "Daddy get you to come and double-check my work? I wasn't aware you were skilled enough already to check the fence line." His voice drips with a gentle sarcasm, as if he's testing my personality type to see if it meshes with his own.

I scoff. "Very funny. Seems like you've already gotten big ideas about me. Let me guess—city girl coming to the country to escape her busy life she can't get a handle on." As soon as I say it out loud, it strikes me as more or less true.

He doesn't say anything as he dismounts from Rosie's back with the fluid motion of someone who's done it a million times. He slips the split leather reins along her neck and folds them adeptly in his wide hands. Rosie stomps her foot on the grass, and Levy gives her a bit of a scratch on the neck. "Want a ride back to the house? I'll lead. You just have to hold on."

I adjust the band on my wrist, twisting it around and around as I roll the idea in my head.

"I'll take that as a no," he says, tipping his hat and starting to lead Rosie away from me.

"I've never been on a horse before," I mumble, the words so quiet I'm not sure they even count as breaking the silence I've held onto for so long.

He hears them, though. "Well then, Rosie's perfect for you. She's used to beginners bumbling around on her back. I promise I won't let her run away with you. At least, not until your second ride."

He lifts his hand to give me the reins, but my body immediately seizes and goes into defensive mode. Shielding myself with both hands, I take a step backward while holding my breath. This type of reaction is the very reason I'm standing in Alabama, seven hundred and thirty-five miles away from the boy who left me this fearful in the first place.

"I'm s-sorry. Defensive reaction."

Levy's eyes are kind but worried at the same time. I've never seen a boy my age show that kind of emotion, and it crashes into me so hard it brings tears to my eyes. I use the back of my hand to scrub at my face casually so he can't catch on.

"Here," he says, holding out his hand, slowly, an invitation to take it only when I'm ready to—and I do. I take his calloused hand in mine, and he guides me forward gently to Rosie's side. "Let's just walk with her. She can get to know your personality; you can get to know hers."

Gathering up the loops, I take the reins in my hand, unsure of what to do next.

"Just walk. She'll follow beside you."

I don't quite believe him, as if walking with a horse must be something innately more difficult than just putting one foot in front of the other. But as soon as I start to move forward with the leather in my hands, Rosie takes a step. Then another. Before I know it, we're walking across the field, Levy in tow.

"So, Morrigan, tell me about you. What really brings you to the Creek?" Levy asks the question as if it's the most nonchalant thing in the world.

To be fair, he doesn't know there's so much history behind my visit, but I also don't feel now is the moment to try and explain it to yet another stranger. Instead, I carefully calculate my path over the grass. The sun hits the blackness of Levy's hair just perfectly from this angle, reflecting little prisms of dark violet and blue.

"For starters, it's just Mo." I readjust the reins in my hands and keep my eyes fixed on Rosie to ensure I'm doing everything right but equally to avoid looking at Levy. "And, I don't know, lots of things I guess."

"Hmmm, let's start with something easier then, *Mo*." His voice lingers on my nickname. "How about this? I'll ask you a question, and then you get to ask me one."

"You already asked yours. So that makes it my turn." I'm happy to have a chance to get the attention off me. "How long have you been working here?"

"A year," he replies with some hesitation. "Ever since I graduated from high school. I always wanted to be a rancher. I'm a competitive reiner as well, and working here for your dad pays for my entry fees and gives me a couple of project horses to work with to bring around for sale in the spring. Now I'm going to ask you the same question again since you gave me a crappy answer. What brings you here, for real?"

He doesn't seem like the type of person to let this go, and clearly, he already has some kind of super-secret intuition about my life.

"Boyfriend, mostly. Well, ex-boyfriend now."

"He the reason you wear the band around your wrist?"

"I guess you could say that."

We shuffle through the longer bits of grass in silence, stopping every once in a while to check a post or rail.

"You going to ask me anything else?" Levy questions, kicking a bit of dust off his boots. He turns to look at me as he walks, giving me a bright smile.

"Oh, right. I guess I'm curious if you grew up here?"

"Sort of. Mom and Dad spent some time in Georgia, but Dad got really into mustang training, and I kind of picked up after him. We work with the horses on a more personal level I think than a lot of ranchers do. Something special about the spirit of a horse. It's not meant to be broken like how the traditional ranchers of the older times work them."

The way he talks about horses is dreamy as if he's moved far away, even though he's still walking beside me.

"That sounds nice."

He takes a beat and looks me over, head to toe. What's he thinking? His eyes and expression give nothing away.

"Don't think I missed that tattoo peeking out from your back when you got out of the truck. There's nothing wrong with that. But there is *something* wrong."

I swallow hard while a little trickle of sweat that has nothing to do with the heat drips down my spine. "You don't know anything about me." The words are lost somewhere between emotions—angry and embarrassed and scared all at once—as I jam the reins back into his hands.

He jumps back from me in surprise, the force of my exchange nearly knocking him off balance. "Morrigan. Shit, Mo—"

I push open the paddock gate, then stomp down the

gravel path I'm only fractionally confident leads toward the house. An errant and annoyed tear crawls down my face, leftover from earlier in the conversation between the two of us, and for the second time in ten minutes, I rub at my presumably red face to get rid of the telltale signs of my overwhelming emotions. I'm an idiot. First day here—the first hour, really—and I'm already in tears because of a conversation with some boy. Thankfully, I have a five-minute walk back to the house, the gravel markers along the paddock lanes leading me to the driveway, and by that point, I've made myself scarce from Levy's gentle eyes. I take a deep breath and open the door as if nothing ever happened between Levy and me.

I guess, in a way, nothing did.

The inside of the house is quaint, well-appointed, and rustic, something that someone might see in a movie if they were researching ranches in Alabama and wanted an idea of what the film set would look like. The open-concept dwelling is all exposed beams and hardwood floors, with leather furniture and fuzzy blankets and industrial lighting. There's an interesting mix of genres in the way the place is decorated. Ultimately, it looks exactly the way I imagined it would when my mother told me I was to spend the summer here. A choice I declined many times until it wasn't a choice anymore.

I kick off my sneakers on the front mat, before I bite the inside of my lip as I pad through to the kitchen.

My father is standing over the coffeemaker like he's never seen the thing before in his life. "I see you're learning quickly." He sticks a little round pod in the top opening of the device. "Looked good up there with

Rosie coming down the drive. We'll change your mind about this place yet."

Stifling a yawn, I don't bother to mention that maybe my mind has already started to change. I'm tired already, and it's only four o'clock.

"Can I get you a coffee? There are all kinds of flavors in the pantry. I wasn't sure what you liked, so I picked up a bunch at the market when I was there this morning."

I consider the offer, but my eyes are heavy. "Actually, I think I might go lie down until supper if that's okay." Another yawn grips me, but I shake it off.

"Your room is at the end of the hall. I already put your suitcase and your other bag on the bed. Closet's empty if you want to unpack some of your things so they don't get too wrinkled. There's also a little present in there for you."

The coffee machine whirs with a familiar sound of Michigan, the appliance the same as the one Mom and I have in our kitchen. It's amusing to me that advanced technology is part of something as old-timey as a ranch. I kind of expected making meals over an open flame with a carcinogenic tin pot. Beans and hot dogs out of a can and all that jazz.

Head held high, faking confidence, I traipse down the hall over smooth floorboards, shuffling my feet as I head toward the end of the corridor to an open door. The space is large and sunny, with a big window at one end, a homey and likely handmade bed gracing the other wall to face out over the lawn. The opposite side of the room has a desk and a little wooden chair. My phone sits on top of the surface, plugged into the wall, obviously something my father took care of himself in order to make me feel connected to the outside world, the city. A patchwork quilt is gathered and wrinkled with the weight of the packages set upon it—my things and a box marked Countryman, the present my father mentioned, presumably.

I unfold the edges of the brown cardboard box. Inside is a pair of brand-new cowboy boots, a medium-colored leather, with detailed, plant-like stitching along the sides and grainy turquoise inserts. It's a nice gesture, a generous effort to make me feel like I fit in here, but one encounter with a horse and a short conversation with a self-proclaimed cowboy doesn't make me any less city nor any more country. I slide the box under my bed without thinking twice about it.

Across the room, my phone dings, and I take it to the bed with me. I pull the quilt back from the pillows at the headboard, crawling in on top of the rest of the sheets and tucking myself in amid the cool central air.

Mom: —How was your flight? Did you make it to the ranch okay?—

Morrigan: —Saw it. Gave it a chance. Is it time to come home now?—

Mom: —These things take a little time, Morrigan. You take care of yourself and say hi to your father.—

I think about telling her I don't see the point when she's probably talking to him just as she's talking to me, but I don't. The reason for their divorce eludes me, but I guess maybe when I'm older I'll be able to understand those types of things. Adult relationships may be more complicated than I give them credit for, though I think my relationship with Fitz was just about as twisted and complicated as it gets.

Morrigan: —I will.—

Mom: —Love you.—

Rolling over to face the wall, I close out the texts with my mother and scroll through my mostly empty messenger application. Only three people are listed in the program: my mother, my father, and Fitz. Everyone else in my life kind of disappeared when things with Fitz started going downhill. Mom called them all fair-weather friends, the kind who stick around when things are good but disappear when times get hard. I don't really blame them. I'd probably be a fair-weather friend to them too if roles were reversed. They didn't understand—I hope they never have to.

I click on Fitz's name, and up pop all the messages we ever sent to each other, little colored bubbles back and forth where most of the abuse I used to believe was love remains. As I look through, all the notes he left about my weight and my face and the way I treated him are there.

Fitz: —Nobody will ever love you the way I do. You know that, Morrigan? You're a slut.—

Fitz: —Maybe if you treated me better, we wouldn't have to have this conversation.—

Fitz: —I do these things because I love you. I want you to be the best version of yourself.—

The messages ring through my head on repeat, as they always do. I don't know why I keep them here, in a spot on my phone where I can quickly access them. Maybe I'm torturing myself on purpose, or perhaps I've heard the words for so long I believe them.

Closing the messenger application, I tuck my phone under the feather pillow with an exaggerated sigh. The thoughts aren't healthy, and missing Fitz isn't healthy, but my brain wants him in such a longing way

21

it still hurts. I promised myself I wouldn't message him anymore, and it's a struggle to keep that promise every single day. So instead, I just hold on to his notes here in my phone where I can pretend we're still talking and maybe he has something nice to say.

Or maybe I'm just afraid of being alone. Afraid he's ruined me. Afraid he's right, and nobody will love me like he has.

Chapter 3

Curling into a ball, I wipe a piece of dust from my eye and try my damnedest to get a little sleep before supper. I must doze in and out because I have these strange, short dreams that pass before me—flying over a burning town, walking down an empty hospital hallway—and suddenly I'm being woken up by knuckles rapping on the door frame of the bedroom. The sound jolts me awake, giving me my second almost heart attack on the ranch.

"Morrigan? I've made supper if you're hungry. Barbecued corn and steaks. The boys are putting away the last of the horses from the trail ride and will join us in about ten minutes."

I stretch out my legs, adjusting my position from the cramped-up circle I was coiled into. Barbecue seems like the perfect first-night-on-a-horse-farm kind of food.

Boys? Like there's more of them? I don't know how many more introductions and questions I can take.

"Okay."

Dad smiles at me and turns back down the hallway, and I shove myself out from underneath the sea of blankets I've worn myself into. A floor-length mirror hangs next to the closet doors to my left, and in it, I spot the most ridiculous case of bedhead, a dirt smudge on my cheek, and rubbed-off eyeliner grazing the sides of my eyes. I'm instantly mortified, scrubbing at my face with a makeup-removing cloth, taking everything off my face because the heat makes it feel five times heavier. Ten minutes later, exactly and on the dot, the contents of my suitcase are strewn across the floor and the bed, cosmetics and hair products thrown around the room like I've lived there all my life.

The smell of cooked meat and vegetables wafts through the open doorway, and I hear the clomp-clomp-*clomp* of cowboy boots treading through the entry and being dropped by the kitchen. Laughter and jovial conversation twist through the still air of the bedroom, Levy, my father, and two other unknown voices each holding their own in a discussion about the farm.

"It always amazes me how far people will drive to come to a ranch. City life can't be all the government's cracked it up to be. Trying to buy up all this land. For what?"

"Apartments, Walmarts, you name it."

"They'll have to fight a lot harder than they are to get this land. When I practiced litigation in Michigan…" My father's voice trails off as the men walk out into the dining area, only picking back up again as I follow my nose down the hall to the scent of old-fashioned home cooking. Mom isn't much of a chef, and neither am I, so I can't quite recall the last time I've had something that wasn't prepackaged or ordered from a takeout menu.

When I get to the room, Dad is standing next to the table, dishing out steaks to Levy and two people I don't recognize. One is tall and thin, older, with a speckled gray beard while the other can't be much more than sixteen if he's even that.

"Ah, Morrigan. Did you have a good rest?" Dad plunks a steak with a little *thwop* on the plate in front of my empty chair. "You've already met Levy. This is Declan and Ranger. These guys all keep the show running smoothly."

Dad points in the men's general direction, saying the names so fast I don't know exactly which one is which.

"Hi, miss," one of them replies, the other shoving a piece of bread in his mouth as if he hasn't eaten in a year. His voice is young like maybe he hasn't hit puberty yet, although judging by the waggling mustache on his face, he definitely has. Though, anyone would look young sitting next to Levy. He just has this older aura about him that makes the rest of us seem like children.

"Hi," I reply, the words quietly coming from somewhere deep in my throat. My father almost seems surprised I've said anything at all, but then again, I guess he doesn't know I spoke with Levy this afternoon.

I place myself across the table from Levy, his eyes watching every move I make like he's a hawk. I'm used to being watched. Fitz did that kind of thing on a regular basis, but there's something different about Levy's eyes on me, and I can't quite put my finger on it. Maybe it's because I want them there, but then I feel bad for the sentiment. I wasn't always a shy person. In fact, there was a time I would have loved being the only girl sitting around all these new guys to figure out. But now, I feel small and out of place.

"How was the trail group other than their very strange ideologies?" Dad passes a serving dish of foil-wrapped corn around the table, starting with me. I grab at one of the packets before realizing the wrapper is hot, and the entire dish goes flying onto the floor, skittering as if the bowl is just as surprised as I am.

I curse but stop halfway through the word because I don't know how my father feels about me swearing at the dinner table. The look on his face tells me not to keep going.

Apologizing, I pick searing corn up with my bare hands, burning them more in the process. "At least it's all wrapped, right?"

"All right, it's fine, Morrigan. Just pass the corn around to Ranger, and we'll say grace before eating." Dad stares directly at Ranger—the younger of the two strangers—who is shoving a second roll in his mouth.

The bowl nearly falls from my hands again. We never said grace up in Michigan after I turned nine. Nobody in our family was even remotely religious, and I think once I told them Jesus didn't make sense, Mom and Dad kind of gave up on the whole charade. Stifling a laugh as if the statement is a joke at my expense, I am quickly forced into an awkward coughing fit when I look up and realize he's serious.

Oh, Jesus Christ—no pun intended—*please* don't make me recite grace.

"Morrigan, since you're our guest tonight, why don't you lead the grace prayer? You must remember the one we used to say back home?"

My heart starts to pound in my chest, and I drop my gaze again down at my steak, the juices leaking out all over the white porcelain dinner plate. Ideas run through my head as to all the ways in which I can get out of this situation, but short of scrambling from the table screaming, there doesn't seem to be anything I can do. Dad sure is pushing the limit here. We're barely talking at all, and he's putting me on the spot for a public blessing.

"Are you sure?" I stare at him, blankly. My mouth opens a bit to say something more, but no sound comes out.

"It's the tradition here on the ranch that the visitor says grace. Now come on. The food's going to get cold. Something short and sweet."

I toy with the bracelet around my wrist as I always do when I'm nervous, and stare down at the tinfoil corn wrapper. Out of the corner of my eye, I can see Levy watching me spin the bracelet around my wrist, over and over, while Ranger and Declan share some kind of glance that tells me to hurry it along because they're hungry.

"I have an idea," Levy interjects, apparently sensing my panic from across the table. "Why don't we have a communal grace? Everyone can add something they feel blessed to have or are thankful for."

"Well, that's a great idea," my dad agrees and begins his contribution to the blessing with reciting the Holy Trinity—Father, Son, and Holy Spirit.

Thank you, I mouth to Levy, and he dips his head as if he hasn't seen my mouth form the words. The edges of his hair cover his dark eyes for just a moment, and I almost look away before he brings his gaze back up to meet mine, winking, as Declan recites a quick thank you to the Lord. I've practically become a professional at keeping my distance from people, never letting anyone get too close, but Levy is definitely going to challenge every obstacle I try to put between us.

Then, suddenly, it's my turn, and I haven't even begun to think about what I'm going to say. "Dear God, thank you for blessing us with this wonderful meal. We appreciate all of the gifts you've given to us on this day and—" There's a pregnant pause in the room, but I don't look up because I suspect either Ranger or Declan or Levy or everyone is staring at me, waiting for me to either find my words or give up. "I g-guess that's everything," I stammer. "Thanks, God. You're great."

Levy snorts audibly, and before I know I'm doing it, my leg extends to kick him under the table.

After supper, night draws in slowly around the ranch, inky rows of bleeding pinks and purples setting over the horizon in the west field. Most of the herd of horses has moved into the distance, seeking nighttime grass and the cooler temperatures, leaving them as tiny, colored specks amid the emerald green of the pasture. The fence line creates ragged shadows on the ground, like crooked fingers reaching across the paddocks for evening air, and I find myself sitting on the back porch in a rocking swing with my socked feet now dirty with dust.

I'm perusing through my phone, no real purpose intended, just scrolling back and forth through the home screen to apps I never use, looking at Instagram posts of people I don't really know. I've deleted Fitz off my following list, mainly due to the requests of my doctors and because I wanted to start the healing process. I thought maybe I could give it a bit of a kick in the ass if I just dumped Fitz out of my life entirely, but my brain still doesn't seem to want to let him go, despite his negative qualities.

The screen door squeaks open, Levy appearing in the entrance with two mugs of coffee. "Deep in thought?" He starts to hand one of the steaming cups over to me, and I reach to take it, but he pulls back for a moment. "Careful now, it's hot," he says in a mocking tone, reminding me of the corn incident.

"Real funny."

Levy takes a seat across from me, sipping at his drink before placing it on a side table. "You want to talk?"

I purse my lips and raise my eyebrow paired with a forced exhale. "There's nothing to talk about."

"Really? Seems like there might be something there worth saying."

"I think you might be projecting your feelings onto me. I have nothing to talk about."

This makes him smile, and his smile softens my hard exterior just a tiny bit.

"You sound like one of those brain doctors, which makes me think maybe the band on your wrist has something to do with it. But if you don't want to tell me, well, you don't want to tell me. I just find sometimes it's easier to talk to a stranger than someone you love."

I presume he means my father, who apparently mentioned my lack of conversation so far.

"You know a brain doctor isn't a technical term?" I take a drink of the hot coffee, a smooth hazelnut flavor washing over my tongue. "They're called psychiatrists."

"I think the technical term here in the South is quacks," he corrects with a smile.

I can't help that I smile back.

"Anyway, I won't keep pushing you. If you want to talk about it, I'm always around."

"Thanks, I'll remember that."

We sit in silence for a second, watching the sun go down, before he pushes himself from the seat and picks up his coffee.

"You don't have to leave." The tone that comes out from me is a little bit desperate, and it strikes me I really don't like being alone. "Okay, look, I do want to talk. Just not about yesterday. Or the day before that. Or any time that can be labeled as the past."

He laughs, a tinkering sound with a gruff undertone. He turns on the heel of his boot, and I'm certain I've already harmed my chance at my first friend here.

"I'm going to get some Kahlúa for my coffee," he says. "You want some?"

"I'm eighteen," I remind him, offering him the chance to change his mind about giving his boss's underage daughter liquor. "How old are you, anyway?"

The question falls from my lips before I have the chance to close my mouth, and Levy puffs out a small bit of breath with a sideways smile.

"And I'm nineteen. Thanks for confirming. Now do you want some Kahlúa or not?"

I don't really know what Kahlúa tastes like, especially not in coffee, but I hold up my mug, and Levy takes it. His fingers brush against my own, and immediately little sparks of electricity flow between us. He must feel it too because he grasps the coffee a little longer than necessary, as if we're magnets stuck together. Heat's there too, but it's dry as the summer sun, and I can't tell if there's an impending thunderstorm or if Levy is just making me hot down in the pit of my stomach.

I'm the one who lets go first, because I think of Fitz and how he's never made me feel this way, and I'm a little bit embarrassed.

"Do you believe in love at first sight, Morrigan?" Levy's voice hangs heavy and warm in the cooling night.

The question might be a rhetorical one, but I feel compelled to answer. "I don't know." A whispered lilt to my voice matches his own. The rocking swing creaks in the tranquility, a little swarm of bats flying over our heads and off into the sunset like airborne shadows.

"I don't know either," he responds with a sigh, turning abruptly toward the screen door and letting himself in the house with no more than a final deep glance into my eyes.

At that moment I notice I've been holding my breath, and I am forced by physiology or nature or whatever controls those impulses to stay alive to do just that. So I breathe, in and out and slowly in a valiant attempt to calm my racing heart. He's asked such a loaded question, with no context, and I am crushed at the thought of it weighing down on me.

Levy takes no time at all to return with the coffees, the smell of them both having changed to something milkier. He passes the blue cup back over to me, and I take a drink from it, the flavor different from how it tasted before, with a serious tone of alcohol. I swear he's dumped more Kahlúa in my mug than anything else.

I swallow the big mouthful and make a face. "Shit, that's strong."

He tastes his own, regaining his spot across the deck from me. "Don't tell me you're not a drinker."

I wait a moment, for emphasis rather than thought. "I'm not really a drinker. My ex-boyfriend didn't like to see me lose myself at parties. He always said I was kind of a nuisance because he'd have to keep an eye on me."

He wrinkles his brow, taking another gulp of the alcoholic coffee. "A nuisance, huh? What did you do when you were drinking?"

"It's more that he didn't trust other people around me, I think. I'm not really sure, to be honest. That's just what he said, and I did my best to respect it. Our relationship worked better that way."

He hums. The darkness starts to take over the porch so much the solar-powered post caps come on. Little freckles of stars appear in the country night, constellations as far as the eye can see, while I swing back and forth on the chair and try not to stare at the way the early moonlight rests on this boy's face.

The screen door creaks open again, sticking a little against the sliders.

"Declan and Ranger are heading off, Levy. You're well past your usual time here. Remember we've got to be up early for the trailer arrival. You might want to pack it in." Dad's voice is both stern and curious, if there's an option to be such things at the same time.

Levy nods, picking up my cup from the deck and rising from his seat. "Nice talking to you, Mo. I'll see you tomorrow. Maybe we can arrange a time for a ride with Rosie as we talked about."

"I'd like that, I think," I admit, my face flushing a little bit hot in the blackness. I presume nobody can see, but I feel the sensation—warm—crawling up the back of my neck and wrapping red fingers around my cheekbones.

Levy disappears into the cavernous opening of the midnight house, brushing past my father with a nod and a simple goodnight. I swear he gives me a little wink, but that might just be my imagination.

Chapter 4

My father takes a chair and scratches it across the stained wood of the deck in an adjustment. He has a glass of something dark and icy in his hand.

"So you and Levy are hitting it off?" Dad takes a sip of his drink as my stomach warms at the name.

"He's nice, I guess." I nod, shifting my weight on the rocking swing and pulling at my socks to cover my legs a bit more. "It's been a little while since I've really had anyone my age to talk to."

Ice cubes clink against the glass of my father's drink. The occasional snort of a horse in the dark punctuates the deep abyss of black. The night sky, in my head, seems darker here than it did in Michigan. Fewer lights pollute the natural world; only dots of twinkling stars and a big ivory moon give a hint of visibility.

"You could invite a friend or two here for a visit this summer if you want," he offers, genuine undertones softening the usual gruffness of his voice. "You don't have to be alone here. This isn't a punishment, Morrigan. It's just a change of pace."

I stifle a laugh.

Dad doesn't seem to be privy to the information, but I lost most of the friends I had when I went off the deep end. My guy friends disappeared almost apologetically while the girls didn't end up saying much at all. I lost more than a boyfriend when my relationship turned sour. I pretty much lost everything, socially—emotionally too. So it's funny, his suggestion to invite a friend or two from home to visit Alabama when they didn't even come to see me in Michigan after things went downhill.

"I'll think about it," I reply, unraveling myself from my seated position. "I'm heading to bed."

Dad hums before swallowing a mouthful. "Night then, Mo."

I'd swear there's a little bit of melancholy in his voice as I slide the patio door open and leave for the indoors, walking over the threshold of the house. In the kitchen, I rinse out the rest of the Kahlúa from my cup and leave the mug upside down in the kitchen sink. Following the balmy yellow light tracing down the corridor leads me to my temporary bedroom complete with all the things I've brought from Michigan in a vague attempt to regain some sense of control. The air is cool, and the night is infinite. As I close the door, flick off the lights, and start to undress, milky stars stand out against the twilight, reminding me that out there, somewhere, Levy is standing under the same night sky and traveling home.

I have no idea when I fell asleep or what time it is when I open my eyes, and I don't bother to check. The sun isn't peeking through the blinds, and the room is still the darkest shade of black it can be; that's enough for me to know I can get a bit more sleep. Tossing and turning, I try to find sleep again, but it evades me as it likes to do, my throat dry with dreams and open-mouthed breathing. Reluctantly, I poke at the screen of my phone, and the light blinds me with the time—five something in the morning. *Ugh.*

I need a drink.

As I open the bedroom door, the warm yellow glow of my phone is gone and replaced by the darkness of the hallway. I don't want to turn on a light and wake up my father, so I use my hand to balance myself the length of the wall to the kitchen with tentative steps. It takes twice as long for me to find my way without tripping over anything in the corridor, and once I make it to the kitchen entrance, I run my fingertips up and down the wooden wall, trying to find a light. Of course, my father has a house where the light switches aren't in the right place, so the illumination of the moon through the window is just going to have to do it. I dig through a cupboard, then another, trying to find the glasses, suddenly regretting not taking the tour Dad offered earlier.

As I turn to open the cupboards to my right, someone clears their throat from the kitchen doorway and flicks on the under-the-cupboard lights. My immediate reaction, after I half jump out of my skin, is to pull at the hem of my shirt to cover as much of my legs as I can.

Levy.

"Looking for something?" he asks, leaning into the doorframe with a cup of coffee in his hand.

"What are you doing here?" I try to bury myself in the corner of the cabinets where maybe he won't be able to see my underwear. The less he can see me, the better.

"I work here."

"It's—" I search for the clock for a second, finding one over my left shoulder. "—5:34 in the morning."

"It is, it is. Which makes you thirty-four minutes late."

"You start at five in the morning?" I say in surprise.

"No, *we* start work at five," he clarifies.

I don't miss the emphasis on the *we*.

"Now, is that what you're wearing, or—?" His smile brightens up the room more than the cupboard lights do. He's apparently enjoying every moment of this, amused at my expense as I stand here on the tile floor with my butt half hanging out.

Forfeiting my water mission, I push past him with my hands tightly grasping the hem of my top, pulling it down tight to my knees.

"Have you really never seen a Western film? Or read a book, perhaps?" he calls behind me as I shuffle down the hall for real clothing. I'm barely paying attention to where I'm going, and as I hit the place where the wall juts out for a linen closet or something equally stupid, I smash my foot on the baseboard.

Good morning, Tin Star Ranch, I think to myself amid curse words. *Thanks for the gentle wake-up.*

Twenty minutes later, the floor-length mirror off to the side of the room shows my hair as being presentable, and I slide on a pair of skinny jeans and a yellow tank top from the top of my bag. I despise that I have to put socks back on, but I do before tugging on my sneakers. They feel like walking on little clouds, the inside of them made to perfectly form to my foot, no breaking in required. When I look up as I go to exit the bedroom, I realize I look a bit like I haven't slept in a week.

The smell of coffee—sans alcohol—wafts through

the house as I head down the hall, back toward the space where it feels like I ate supper only minutes before, and Dad and Levy are planning the day over coffee and a slapdash breakfast.

"We'll have to keep an eye on the weather and the wind. See what direction things are going to go in. Right now, there are ten forest fires burning up in Valley Heights and Stockton."

The conversation halts once I'm spotted, and I have no idea what either of them is talking about. Ranch stuff.

"Morning," my father greets me, handing over a steaming cup. "Trailer should be here any minute. We'll unload the horses into the empty small field to the south, then get started on daily chores. Levy's offered to show you around a bit, Mo. Seems like you guys have made a fast friendship. I'm glad to hear it."

I nod and look into my coffee mug, avoiding Levy's gaze. The embarrassment from my half-naked kitchen quest this morning hasn't quite worn off enough to make comfortable eye contact.

"Declan is off at the auction in Guysborough until Tuesday, and Ranger's working on his home ranch today, so it's just us," Levy explains after taking a bite of an overcooked bagel, the whole thing sounding like a bit of a foreign language. "I've already done the feeding, so it's just stalls, swapping turnout, that sort of thing. Plus, we'll probably want to have a good look over the new crew to see what we've got to work with. Oh, and there's a trail ride at ten. I'll tack up Rosie for you, and you can ride along if you want."

"Sounds like a good plan for the day to me." My father places his empty, crumb-filled plate in the sink as

I take the first sip of my coffee. "On that note, I spot someone coming up the drive. Might as well go out and meet them. Put that cup down, Mo. Horses come first."

I nearly drop the whole mug on the floor with a second stifled yawn. I'm not sure how I'm supposed to function all morning with hardly any caffeine, but by the time I go to complain, Levy and my father are already halfway down the driveway, front door left ajar and waiting for me. I do as Dad says and follow them half-heartedly. The day is hot, but there's smoke on the horizon, or maybe it's a deep fog. It's hard to tell when I'm barely awake.

The long trailer kicks up dust as it travels underneath the Tin Star Ranch sign and parks itself in front of the house with a mechanical sigh. A gruff-looking man pulls himself from the driver's seat of the black truck, and he shakes both my father's and Levy's hands as I approach. They're already deep in conversation by the time I can overhear, a trait that seems more and more typical of my time on the property. I always miss the first little bit of everything.

"…down in Pagosa, all the way over. Had to drive around, so it took a couple of extra hours. But they're here. Might need a good leg stretching. Speaking of leg stretching, how's that black colt I brought up for you last time? I'd like to have a peek at him while I'm here."

"Growing like a weed—long legs on him," my father notes. "Good bloodlines some way back, nice and calm. Levy and Ranger have been working on the trail with him."

Levy picks up a lead line from the front bench, giving me a soft shove as he murmurs to me under his breath. "They'll talk forever. Come see the horses with me."

I smile and follow him to the truck, a dirt and dust-stained hauler attached to the back and filled with snorts and foot stomping.

"They're ready to come out." Levy laughs, flipping the line over his shoulder and undoing a large bolt on the side door. "We've got six this time, a good, full-size load from Jasper Hole. Five geldings and a mare."

He turns a few more levers and unclips some hooks, and suddenly a ramp lowers from the trailer, six tired faces appearing over small stall doors. There's the scent of wood chips and hay, all scattered over the rubber floor, and a little gray horse with a bold white face gives us a curious nicker.

"Want to name them? Usually whoever unloads gets to pick." He removes a line from the first horse's halter and attaches his own lead.

"Oh God, I don't know what to name a horse."

He holds the blue cotton line out to me, and I take it without thinking as if holding a horse is the most natural thing in the world for me to be doing.

"Hold this girl while I undo the back door, and you can think about it. Then we'll back her out nice and easy."

Levy pops out of the trailer and disappears around the corner, while the gray gives me a gentle push with her nose. I slide my hand up and down over the white of her face, tiny loose hairs falling all over my bare arm and tickling my skin before she turns her head away and pulls a mouthful of hay from the net with vigor. There are a few moments of banging at the back behind the horses, and I watch as their ears turn toward the sound and away from it, listening with a bit of impatience for their impending freedom. Then suddenly sunshine pops through the opening as Levy lowers the second ramp, easing the slope down to touch the drive. The gray gives a sudden pull on the line, starting to back out without my permission, but the restraint and hesitation of my hand stops her in her tracks just as Levy reaches around me to take the horse back.

"I'll take her off slowly, so you might want to go stand off to the side. These are slaughter horses, and they're bound to be edgy. I don't know exactly how they're going to react. It might be best for you to think about naming them from farther out of the way."

I nod. The last thing I need on my second day at the ranch is to get stepped on or kicked by a wild horse.

Levy unloads the gray with a skill I never knew I didn't have, guiding the horse over the ramp and down onto the settling dust of the driveway. The very second her hooves hit the dirt, she shies away from the trailer, pulling him toward the grass of the field.

"Easy, easy," he croons, keeping a solid pressure on the line. His muscles pop on his shoulders as he struggles to hold back the thousand-and-then-some-pound horse who is having a fit, and I back myself up against the wall of the trailer in order to do my best to stay out of the way. The gray seems like an entirely different animal. While soft and gentle in the trailer, now she appears unbeatable. However, within thirty seconds, Levy has all legs back on the ground and the horse standing stock-still on the dirt road. It's an amazing thing to watch, and I immediately comprehend why my father would want to keep someone like Levy around.

"That one has a lot of spirit," my father calls, chuckling as he pokes his head over from his conversation with the truck driver. "South field, let her have a run."

Out of the corner of my eye, I see Levy smile at me, but I can't keep my eyes off the horse.

"Come for a walk with me? Just—maybe stay a horse length away from us until we figure out what she's going to do."

"She's not going to do anything," I say as if I'm suddenly an expert on the subject. Levy raises an eyebrow, and I bite my bottom lip. "She just got taken away from a place she was used to, and sure, it wasn't the best situation, but she didn't know any better. Now she's been dropped here in this new place with new people and noises and smells. She just needs some time."

Sympathy sets in behind Levy's eyes. I'm almost positive he knows it wasn't just the horse I was talking about. We stay quiet for a while, walking around the ranch and letting the powerful horse take in her new surroundings. She's nothing like Rosie—wilder, more tempestuous—and then it hits me, a perfect name.

"Stormy. Her name is Stormy," I blurt.

"Stormy. I like it." He nods as if I'm not possibly the weirdest person on the planet for just randomly yelling out a name for the horse.

We travel along the center of the property with Stormy in tow, the horse having exhausted herself from her tantrum and traipsing along the emerald blades of grass with an occasional sneaky mouthful. The sun beats down an early morning heat on the three of us, the air murky with what I now recognize as far-away smoke on the horizon. The gray clouds billow up into almost wispy nothingness, but I can smell the acrid scent of burning as if someone's having a campfire or a birthday party way off in the distance. So far it's barely perceptible.

"You can smell it too, huh? I think the horses know something's not quite right." Levy breaks our silence with a statement on exactly what I've been thinking.

"What is it?"

"Forest fire. They're burning all over the state. It's been a long, dry season so far. Don't worry, though. We've been keeping an eye on things, and they're under control. We've got some great firefighters here, and it's not the first time something like this has happened."

I can't help but become a little bit nervous, but I shove the feeling deep down inside of me where I keep my guilt about liking Levy. "Well, that's good to know, then. Under control. I guess they always are until they aren't."

"You're so positive, Morrigan." He pops the latch to the empty field and pushes his way through with Stormy, before pulling off the horse's halter and letting her go.

A few seconds of nothingness pass where Stormy just stands amid the cropped grass and stares at us with her warm, brown eyes as if she's waiting for something to happen. When nothing does, it's like a light goes on, and she recognizes that she's able to run—and when she does, boy does she ever take off. She swings her mane, kicking her heels in the air, stretching out her back legs so high it's as if she's trying to push the sun right out of the sky. With a final twist of her body, she flat-out gallops over the hilltop to leave Levy and me in her dust.

Levy hops up on the fence, balancing on the wooden beam as he watches Stormy find her place here. I follow suit, using the bottom piece of fencing to hoist myself to the top one.

There's something humbling about watching a horse suddenly comprehend freedom, and the cognizance of this makes me wonder what Stormy saw in her life before Tin Star Ranch to make her so skittish and worried.

"She was abused," Levy says, quietly like he's unsure he should say it out loud. "You can tell by the way she looks at you."

I can't tell if he's only talking about the horse or if there is something deeper in the sentiment—something that says he's seen that exact same damaged look in my eyes too.

Chapter 5

My day is long and hard as I learn the ins and outs
of the ranch, help where I can, and stand watch where I
can't figure things out. Later, much later, into the
evening after the horses are fed and three trail rides
have returned, I shower the hard day's work off my
tired body and head to the kitchen for some tea. There's
a note from Dad on the counter.

Mo,

*Headed into town to pick up a part for the truck.
Be back soon.*

Dad

I sit on the porch in the swinging chair, my new
favorite spot to rest, and sip my tea, reading a few
pages of a science fiction book I found on a shelf in the
living room. My eyes keep wandering down the
driveway. I'm waiting for the headlights to appear or
the sound of tires on gravel to echo through the quiet
air, but the minutes tick by and still no sign of Dad. The
silence settles in, and my chest tightens as the night
grows duskier, the sensation of being truly alone in
Alabama taking over. Branches creak in the light
breeze, but the noise isn't enough to make me forfeit
my spot on the swing, and so I fight with my anxiety in
order to appear normal to exactly nobody.

Craving some kind of interaction to trick myself
into thinking I'm not alone, I text my mom, but she

doesn't respond. I scroll through social media, but my dwindling friend lists and news feeds don't offer much for distraction, only offering me pictures of things other people are doing, and mostly famous people I don't really know at that. A few minutes flip by on the screen, and I reopen the messenger app to check if my mother responded, and there it is. Taunting me. Begging me to open it. The message thread between me and Fitz.

I was supposed to delete it, but I never did. I've never been able to bring myself to do it. Then, before I realize what's happening, my fingers are gently swiping over the screen to type a message.

Morrigan: —Hey, I was just thinking about you.—

Staring at the message and the blinking screen, I backspace over and over again until the note disappears into cyberspace.

Morrigan: —What are you up to?—

I don't hit send, instead opting to close the app. Admittedly, it takes me a little longer than it should to comprehend I shouldn't be texting Fitz or even considering it. And then I realize, why send a text when I could hear his voice? I know I shouldn't, but the part of me that misses him, though fractional compared to the part of me that hates him, is strong enough. It only takes one hole in the protective exterior walls to take down an entire ship. For me, it's him. Fitz is the crack in the walls that will let the danger in and leave me submerged once and for all.

I don't try to talk myself out of it. Just the opposite, in fact. My thumb hovers over the call button, and butterflies dance in my stomach. I want to call. I want to hear his voice. I want this.

I take a deep breath and hit the call button. My heart pounds over and over again in my chest, slamming against my rib cage as I bite my bottom lip. What will I say? What will he say? But the phone doesn't ring. Instead, a high-pitched error tone and a robotic female voice crackle through the line.

"We're sorry. The number you have dialed has been disconnected. Goodbye."

My phone slips through my sweating palm, and it crashes to the floor of the porch. I choke on the tears I try to swallow back, my body shaking with rage, grief, anger—and regret. I should have known better than to think I'd be able to hear Fitz's voice and everything would be okay. I should have known better than to try and bring him back into my life. Someone up there in the sky, be it God or whatever the truth is, is screwing with fate and making it so I can't incur any more mistakes. At least not soon.

I consider picking up the phone and throwing it over the fence into one of the pastures for a horse to crush the device into pieces, but I don't. Instead, I rub the sneaky tears from my face, leave the book on the swing, and slam my way into the house. I know there's a bottle of Kahlúa somewhere in the house, and I'm determined to find it and maybe dull the pain I'm feeling. As I track my way into the kitchen, however, the bottle is empty on the countertop from the night before, piled with beer cans in a mound ready for recycling. So much for that idea.

A dark feeling comes crashing over me, and it's something painful and familiar. Alone in the house, I'm not sure how to deal with it until I remember I haven't taken my medication since I arrived here at the ranch.

I'm a couple of days behind, so no wonder I'm feeling generally off. I fill a cup from the cabinet halfway with water and traipse down the hallway to my temporary bedroom. There on the nightstand are my bottles of pills, waiting for me to remember them. It took me a long time to understand having to take these doesn't make me weak, no matter how hard my inner demons were chanting otherwise. I unscrew the tops and shove the medicine in my mouth as fast as I can before more destructive thoughts prevail, and then crawl under the covers and wait for something to swallow me whole.

Amazingly, it's sleep that takes me, and I fall into something dark and dreamless.

Five in the morning comes around much too soon, my head pounding while my stomach does cartwheels and throws metaphorical rocks around my insides. The feeling is similar to waking up after a long night of drinking, only this isn't a regular hangover. It's an emotional one. I've had too many feelings the night before, and now I'm paying for being human.

"Mo?" Dad calls through the door, the worry in his voice seeping through. "Are you okay?"

I don't answer, and he doesn't push the subject, but I can tell by his short sentences with awkward pauses that he doesn't want to leave me by myself.

"Okay. Well, we're going to be out on the ranch. You know where to find us when you're ready—if you're ready."

I pull the covers over my head and argue with my antidepressants, begging for them to start working faster. The hurt I felt when I heard that dial tone and out-of-service message is indescribable, the kind of pain that has to get worse before it can get better.

Partly, because it means Fitz has made me a part of his past, while he's still very much a part of my present, even if I wish he wasn't. When it was time, I wanted to be the one to sever the final tie—and he took that away from me, the way he took everything else.

But mostly, I'm mad at myself. I feel guilty that I've taken so many steps forward to take a giant leap back. The hollow tone on the other end of the line solidified that the last connection I had to Fitz is gone.

It's as unnerving as it is relieving.

I must fall back asleep again because a time goes by where I don't remember anything. It's either that, or I've been staring at the underside of the quilt for hours before there's a tiny break in the way I feel.

The sun peaks in the sky, brightening my whole room in a natural light that indicates it's around noon, but I'm unsure of the exact time. I drag myself from underneath the warmth of the comforter before changing and running a brush through my hair. This will force me to put one foot in front of the other to at least go and sit outside so I don't seem like I'm not participating in farm life any longer. Participating a little bit was on my list of things to do, and my father and Levy are trying so hard to include me it seems almost rude not to bother with them for the entirety of a day. Unfortunately, my head still feels like I'm underwater, and I rummage around in my luggage for a bottle of Tylenol. When I find it, I pop a few into my mouth and swallow them dry.

I make it to the front porch, and the journey almost seems like a miracle. I crawl onto the swing and wrap my feet under my blanket from last night. The science fiction book is still split down the middle, waiting for me to finish it. As I sit and breathe and think, the silhouette of a man and a horse grows up over the hill, spotlighted by the brilliant sun in such as way that it blocks who the shape belongs to. The shape starts to blot out the rays behind them, and soon I can see Levy under his familiar black hat, mounted on Rosie who walks at her usual calm, slow speed.

He waves to me, and I return the motion even though my hand feels like it's made out of lead. A few moments later, he directs Rosie toward the porch, dismounts while she's still walking, and heads up the steps while leaving Rosie free-range near the house.

"She won't go anywhere?" I ask as Levy leans into the railing.

"Not anymore. She's used to us now. Comfortable. She knows she can trust us and that we're doing what's best for her. She used to fight us though, not hard, but enough to let us know we had to play by her rules. So what do you think?" he asks. The widened look in my eyes must tell him I have no idea what he asked me because he smiles and repeats the question. "Ready to give Rosie a chance? Take a ride back to the stable?"

"Easy, cowboy. A girl can't just hop up on a horse and hope for the best."

"Tell that to the eight-year-olds who do it at birthday parties." He raises an eyebrow, and his voice is playful.

"Are you challenging me?" I try to match his tone.

"Perhaps."

My heart thinks about it—really thinks about it. I want to jump out of the swing, run across the porch, swing my leg up over Rosie, and gallop into the sunset. But my brain says no. It tells me to stay here on the porch, safe and sound with my heavy heart and cloudy mind.

"I can't." My voice is low, heavy with the fear of trying something new.

"Only one way to find out." Lifting a hand, holding it out, palm up, he waits for me to take it. His eyes lock deeply into mine, waiting for an answer, and I take a deep breath and place my hand in his. I have no idea what I'm getting myself into, but all I know is I can't sit here any longer.

He guides me gently down the steps and across the flower garden row to Rosie's side. "Left foot in the stirrup, hands on the horn. Give a little hop and swing over. I'll be here to help give you a boost. She's only barely a horse, but she'll feel bigger when you're on her back."

I stick my sneakered foot into the leather, stretching my thigh muscle, and place my hands where Levy guides them. His skin is rough against mine, calloused from years of hard outdoor work, but the touch is conservative as if he's worried I might hit him again.

"All right, give a little jump." He tosses the reins over Rosie's chestnut neck and places his hands on my sides.

Little shivers of anticipation slide over me, from the spot he's touching me down to my toes, and I haul myself up into Rosie's saddle rather well, if I do say so myself. Once I sit up tall, like I've seen the Olympic riders do on their mounts, Levy's words echo in my head. Rosie really does seem taller from up here. And I'm nervous, suddenly, but I'm sitting on a horse, just like I really did always want to do.

"You okay up there? You look like you're going to faint."

"I'm fine," I squeak, grasping at the horn of the heavy saddle. "I've just—I've never been on a horse, and I've always wanted to be on a horse. I didn't really expect to be riding one this summer, let alone so soon."

"Just wait until she starts walking." He laughs, taking the reins down off Rosie's neck. "Just sit up tall, push your heels down, and try to relax. Deep breaths. You look good up there."

My face flushes again, but I don't have a chance to respond before he urges Rosie into a quiet walk, her shifts in weight guiding me forward and back with each step.

"Oh my God…" I falter. "This was literally my dream for years."

We take about twenty steps before I'm comfortable at the walk, and my daring nature takes over, and I let go of the horn. My hands are shaking from the pressure I've put on the leather, but something about sitting up there in the sky on Rosie's back makes me feel like nothing else in the world can touch me, not Fitz, not my thoughts, not anything. I'm empty and relaxed and happy I let my heart win—wild heart, as it may be.

The space between us grows so silent that in some ways it's overwhelmingly loud, and I feel the need to try to fill the void.

But I don't. I like the quiet. I like the nothingness we have between the three of us.

Rosie sneezes. The long grass tickles at her legs and belly.

Levy pushes open the gate near the stables and guides Rosie and me through. I'm almost a little bit sad we're back so quickly. I was just starting to get the hang of it. He halts her near the door, holding her reins in one hand and turning to stare up at me. Before responding, I kick my feet out of the stirrups and hop off the little mare, sneakers hitting the ground with a thud. I almost fall over, but his hand finds my hip and steadies me.

"What's the tattoo of?" he asks in a velvet voice that makes me aware he's not going to let me dodge the question forever.

"Maybe I'll show you sometime." I grin before I brush past Levy and walk toward the path that leads to the log house.

"Promise me that one?"

I pause, turning to him for a second, thinking of our conversation earlier—the way he challenged me.

"Only one way to find out." I turn back down the dusty path. "Thanks for the ride, cowboy."

When I get back to the house, Dad is sitting on the stairs of the porch, drinking some kind of iced-tea-looking concoction, his hat resting on his knee. I plunk down on the wooden step beside him, my legs feeling a little wobbly.

"Can I ask you something?" Dad swirls his drink so the ice clinks against the glass.

"I guess so." I try to wipe the ridiculous grin off my face.

"Do you want to go home?" His voice cracks a bit, but he clears his throat and regains his control. "Are you ready to go home already?"

I pick at a splintering piece of wood on the porch and think about his question. I do. I want to go home. But the real question isn't if I want to go home—it's why.

The more I think about it, the more the answer reveals itself to me. I have no reason to want to go back, except for my mother. Other than that, my friends are gone. My boyfriend is now my ex-boyfriend, and he either blocked me or changed numbers. School is over. So I think long and hard about it and realize—I don't want to go back. I thought I did. All this time I could've been enjoying the ranch and the view and this new place at a hundred percent, I still had one foot in Michigan.

Not anymore.

"I rode a horse today," I say, allowing myself to smile so widely I almost can't get the words out correctly.

"Is that so?" My father places his drink on the porch next to him.

"I'd like to do it again tomorrow. And the day after that. And a few weeks from now too."

Dad's eyes brighten in a hopeful fashion. "Well, in that case, Mo, if you're going to stick around, I want you to take the lead on Stormy's care. She's yours. You make the calls."

There's a knot in my throat, and I have to cough once to clear it out. "Really? Are you sure? But I know nothing about horses."

"You'll learn. Between us, we can teach you the basics. It doesn't seem like Levy would mind."

"Looks like I'm going to be breaking in those new boots you bought me after all." I look up at him with my hand over my eyes, shielding the soft glare from the orange light of the afternoon sun. "Maybe I should go try them on to see if they fit."

Dad picks up his glass and takes a sip. "Something tells me they will."

Chapter 6

Something about Stormy drew me in since the moment I saw her, and I am thrilled when my father announces to everyone at dinner that I'll be responsible for her daily care over the course of the summer. Under his watchful eye, along with the supervision of Levy, Stormy grows friendlier every day, a growth that surpasses even my own.

We leave the horses out in the south field for almost a week where they nibble down the grass to stubs and chase each other around in the greenery. My father calls it giving them a rest period, time to get used to the sights and sounds and smells of the property and everything else new around them. I never really thought before about horses being as sensitive as they are, but I come to understand it very quickly when I move too fast around them to fill water troughs, and they all scatter up the hill. They're a little bit like me in that way. The six of them band together like their lives depend on it—though maybe in some circumstances they really would have—and by the following weekend, Levy and I name them all.

Stormy, Lex, Rebel, Teddy, Indy, and Chance.

In between his chores and the scheduled trail adventures, Levy was good enough to take me out for more led excursions on Rosie, even allowing me to join in on a couple of trail rides up through the woods and over the deserted plains of Colbourn Creek. The actual namesake is all dried up now, not much more than a divot in the land where water used to run through, but people still flock from places near and far to walk a borrowed horse through a place that now mainly resembles a desert wasteland.

To be fair, life looks so much different from the back of a horse. I enjoy the view from calm and steady Rosie despite the sights becoming repetitive; after three or four trips I've even started memorizing the path. Naturally, I get to thinking that maybe by the end of the summer, I'll be able to lead these rides with Stormy.

Daydreaming comes easy on the ranch, and more days than not, I leave my cell phone in the bedroom with no messages on it. The only people I want to talk to other than my mother are already all gathered in one place, and there's so much to do once I learn to clean stalls and feed horses that it takes up most of my day. I don't mind really. I'm getting a tan, and my hair is turning more blonde from the sun, but mostly I enjoy spending the time with Declan, Ranger, and especially Levy, working on the farm, and getting horses ready for their day's plans.

Sundays are quiet in comparison to all the other days of the week. It's a rest day for the horses with no trail rides scheduled, and therefore nobody from the public meandering around the property. I'm dragging the heavy, black hose over to the south pasture buckets when Stormy comes to the fence, giving me a little snuffle with her nose. She's more than well aware that I have a piece of carrot in my pocket, stolen from the feed room in the barn, and she wants it desperately.

Levy's shown me how to hand-feed the horses with

my palm flat, and so I place the baby carrot stick in my hand, and Stormy lips it out with an orange-slobbered crunch. This has been our routine for a few days now. If she comes to greet me, she gets a treat. Levy says this is a good way to create a positive association, and it seems to be working.

I give her a pat on the neck, watching the clouds approaching in the distance. The fires are still raging across the state, and over the last few days at dinner, Dad's said grace to the tune of protecting us from the devastation that's overrun many other parts of neighboring towns. He says any day we could get an evacuation order, but I try not to worry any more than necessary because he knows this place much better than I do.

But still, my body tenses up when I get a nose full of smoke, and Stormy snorts out the dirty air the second Levy approaches. His boots crunch on the dry ground, approaching from the side door of the stable, and he leans over the fence to watch me struggle with the watering.

"Think you want to hop on her today after church?" he asks, a casual tone to his voice.

I nearly spray water all over myself, instead squirting Levy with the end of the hose. "Church? I didn't know that was something that was going to happen today. I haven't been to church since—I don't even know when."

Levy shakes the water off his boots, droplets fading into the dirt or the air. It's hard to tell which. "I kind of thought you'd have figured out that church on Sundays was a thing in the country. I mean, we have been saying grace in front of you for a week now."

"I guess I never really thought about it," I admit, adjusting the water flow back into the trough. Levy chuckles, a sound I've gotten so familiar with that I know it better than I know my own.

"Papers say she's trained—was a reiner back in the day. Could be a fun horse for you to learn a thing or two on."

"Sounds like she's going to be a fun horse for you," I quip, turning off the nozzle. "Remember, I've ridden a horse about six times now. I'm not exactly qualified for a horse like that."

"You can walk and jog. That's important. You know the basics, and you've picked them up quickly. I think it's about time you took your project horse for a little spin."

"After church, then." I nod. "I trust you're going to be there to laugh at me when I fall on my ass."

"With so much pleasure, I can't even begin to describe." Levy graces me with a signature smirk before turning on his heel to head to the barn.

I take one look back at Levy as he enters the stable, his black shirt hugging his well-developed muscles in all the right places. I smile, thinking he has drawn me out of my shell more in a handful of days' time than anyone has been able to in months. A little daydream persists where I'm confident enough to tell him how much I enjoy being around him when Stormy headbutts me for another carrot, but my pockets are empty.

"What do you think?" I ask the horse, turning my attention back to her. "After church, we're going to go for a ride. And you'd better be as well-trained as Levy seems to think you are because we both know I have no idea what I'm doing."

Stormy ignores me and dunks her muzzle in the trough, taking a long and noisy drink.

An hour later, I find myself in a pew next to my father and the entirety of Colbourn Creek, sweating profusely due to the lack of air conditioning in the parish. The air is electric, thunderstorms getting ready to roll in based on the blackish skies in the distance. I've put on the nicest outfit I packed, a plain black skirt and a purple sleeveless top, and I can't help but keep pulling at the hems of all the clothing in an attempt to make the fabrics lie differently and not stick so awkwardly to my body in the heat. It doesn't help that I can feel Levy's eyes pressing into me from a few rows back, and when I peek over my shoulder, he gives me the tiniest of winks. I suspect the sensation I get from the gesture is forbidden in church, and that only makes me feel it more.

I haven't missed the looks he gives me and the feelings that pass through me when he gives me that southern, charming half smile, or looks at me with his eyes tilted down under his dark, brimmed hat. I'm not denying we have some kind of connection, but I've been purposely ignoring them. Swallowing back any human emotion that surfaces in fear that if I let one emotion take over, all the emotions will take over. It's easier to shut them all off, no exceptions.

And then I think of Fitz, and a burning sensation rises through my abdomen and chest with guilt—the one emotion I haven't been able to control.

"In the name of the Father, the Son, and the Holy Spirit."

The priest makes the sign of the cross on his body, while I take a deep breath and hold, trying to curb the anxiety I feel at my core. I try to follow along with a shaking hand while he makes his way across the altar to a small podium.

"As I welcome you all here today, I would like to make note that our neighbors are in a state of crisis. Fires have started taking over more nearby towns while being carefully tended to by the brave men and women of our Alabama fire brigades. I have been told rain is in the forecast for this week, and a number of the blazes have been contained to nonresidential areas. This is good news, and I would like for us to take a moment to thank the Lord for his consideration."

The congregation bows their heads as if everyone is a puppet on the same string, except for me of course because I'm unfamiliar with the custom. By the time I figure out what I'm supposed to be doing in the midst of the quiet, the priest has restarted his homily with a bit on forgiveness. I only half listen to the things he is saying, my mind a little distracted by dirty thoughts that shouldn't be allowed in a church. Breathing in through my nose and out through my mouth, I try to calm myself down before my internal struggle becomes external. The room starts to spin as I squeeze my eyes shut, only I'm not in the church anymore. In my head, I'm in the barn with Levy, and we're doling out the suppertime feed, multi-colored buckets scattered along the floor of the grain room with names emblazoned on the sides. My bubbled writing scrawls Chance's name on a green bucket when Levy scoops a mound of pellets, the sound of the grain in the barrel echoing repeatedly with each cupful.

"You know what I want?" Levy asks with a casual tone, dropping a capful of feed supplement into the bucket labeled *Rosie*.

"What's that?" I cap the permanent marker and place it on the back shelf, leaning over Levy's shoulder and smelling the scent of shaving cream mixed with hay.

"You."

The dream version of Levy grabs me by the waist, whipping me around against the grain barrel. His eyes are sparkling with a passion I don't recognize from any of my interactions with Fitz, and I know I'm making up the facial expressions in my head because everything gets a little bit fuzzy as my imagination plays catch-up with my own experiences.

"What about me?" I ask, adeptly slipping my fingers together around the small of Levy's back. He feels strong against me, pressing my thighs into the metal container, and the pressure from his body makes my heart feel strange, itchy.

"I want you. All of you, Morrigan." Levy leans in, his lips tickling the fragile hairs on my neck before he says my name again.

"Morrigan?"

"What, Levy?" The moment turns blurry around the edges.

"Morrigan?"

The name is stronger now, but it is accented by sudden pain, a thump along my entire body that starts at my knees and runs up to my head. The combination of the sound and the sensation bring me crashing down to earth; I'm twirling out of my own head, cascading back into the tiny church and the heat and the bodies all cramped in. It takes me a solid ten seconds to open my eyes and realize I'm lying on the floor with my father,

Levy, Ranger, Declan, and about fifty other people I don't know standing over me. My skirt is gathered above my knees from where I've fallen, and the only thing I can think about is hoping Levy can't get a look at my polka-dotted underwear from his position by my feet.

If I'm not imagining the budding possibilities between us, I'd prefer his first impression of my undergarments be better chosen than this moment.

"Morrigan? Are you okay?" My father's voice is low and careful as if the gentle tone can heal my wounded pride.

A throbbing pain washes over my body, the bones in my knees hurting from where I've apparently banged them on the tile, and my cheek hot with the red slap of the wooden pew where I smashed my face.

I roll to one side, trying not to meet Levy's worried gaze. "I'm fine. I'm sorry." A cup of water materializes over my head, and I take the glass gingerly before drinking to the bottom. "I guess I just got too warm."

A collection of older ladies with large hair cluck together, their tongues making the sound of concerned hens.

"Can you stand?" My father reaches out his hand, and I take it, wobbling a little with the lopsided assistance. Of course, Levy notices the issue immediately, and he gathers by my other side to balance me out. My head is reeling, the world still blurred around the edges, but I manage to get to my feet and allow myself to be dragged out of the church, down the aisle, and into the gray Alabama morning like the gigantic moron I am.

Who lets themselves daydream their mind into a

frenzy like that? Fitz's voice in my head echoes negative words and slurs and mean remarks about the type of person I am and the fashion in which I am always trying to attract attention to myself.

"Do you want me to take her back to the ranch?" Levy asks my father as they haul me to the truck at the nearest end of the parking lot. "Air conditioning and some ice packs ought to get her cooled off and ready for the rest of the day."

"Are you okay with that, Mo? Levy'll take you back to Tin Star?" He says the second part like it's a question even though I don't think it is. "I've got to stay here to take some of the older ladies back to their care facility once the mass is over."

I rub at my eyes with the hand that isn't draped around Levy, the feeling of his body only intensifying my dizziness and frustrating the words I hear from Fitz's distant mouth.

"Yeah," I murmur, not able to formulate any additional words. My legs feel like jelly, and I'm pretty sure if I try and get any more words out of my mouth, I'm going to use up all the energy I have left that I'm using to stand. A couple of fuzzy moments later, I'm buckled into Levy's truck, a fresh pine scent surrounding me, and the door slams closed with a crack. The upholstery smells like Christmas, and I close my eyes to shut out the prickling feeling in my fingertips and toes as if my vision has something to do with it all.

I think I might cry, but I don't want to. I don't want to cry in front of Levy because I don't want him to know just how truly broken I am, in all parts, everywhere.

Chapter 7

Levy turns the truck engine over and slowly starts to pull out onto the road. Cool air blasts from the vents, hitting me square in the face and right over my legs, while I focus more intently on breathing than I ever have in my life. Gradually the pixelated feeling fades, my eyes clear, and I become coherent, though I can't help wishing the last ten minutes from the church until now were nothing more than a bad dream.

"Never a dull moment with you, is there?" Levy smirks, turning the wheel hand-over-hand as we pass underneath the Tin Star Ranch sign.

"Very funny." The words groan out of my mouth like thick soup, all stuck to my throat along the edges.

We cruise up the gravel in silence, save for the radio churning out an old-timey song where a man is crooning about losing the woman he loves to someone else. I shimmy my skirt down as long as I can make it, trying to cover my poorly-shaven knees and pale tan lines. Levy seems to be pretending not to notice my embarrassment over the whole situation. He barely stops the truck before I hop out of the passenger's side door, waving a thank you before teetering in through the front door, the screen slamming behind me as tears stream down my face. Fitz's voice might just haunt me forever, and a part of me doesn't want to let that go. It's a sick obsession, a painful one at that, and I can't help but wonder if I just spit out our story to someone, somewhere, if that might make the poison of his words disappear.

I am weak by the time I get into my bedroom and shut the door, leaning against the wooden slab with heaving shoulders and tears like rainwater down my face. I'm a disaster of the worst kind, finally understanding why my mother decided to send me away, and I throw myself on the bed. My phone bounces off the pillowcase, coming to rest faceup on the crinkled quilt.

Wiping the tears off my cheeks with the back of my hand and soaking my wristband, I try my hardest to ignore the silent screams of the device before ripping off my stupid skirt. A tape plays over and over again in my head, reminding me both that I'm an idiot and also a dynamic slob, and I kick off my shoes in frustration, sending them flying into the farthest wall with a bang before I pull on a pair of dirty jeans.

Strong emotions always do something to me. They turn me into some kind of animal, hijacked by the very line between nature and nurture. The follow-up sensation hits me desperately, a dragging-down feeling of needing Fitz, the painful reminders that he exists, and his pretty words he always manages to use to make me feel something, anything.

An hour passes.

I pick up the phone daintily and flip to the messages application where I've kept some of Fitz's best messages. The ones where he doesn't treat me like I'm a piece of meat, the others where he actually says something that could be construed as gentle and kind.

Fitz: —I love you, you know that? You're my

world.—

Fitz: —I want you to be the best version of yourself, Morrigan.—

Fitz: —Everything I do, I do because of you. I do for you. I do for us.—

At the moment, all these notes, these tiny little sentiments in text message format, all seem particularly beautiful and special. And the unsteady current version of myself wants that back, wants to take the steps behind and throw me into my former life. A life where I don't feel things for charming people like Levy who are all good, who don't faint in church or dump hot food all over themselves or use physical violence and snarky words as a reflex for personal protection.

I think about clicking Fitz's name on my phone again. I consider, for a long while, dialing his number and listening to the error message where there should be a ringtone over and over and over again until it doesn't hurt anymore.

So I start typing a miniature poetic novel in the little white box below the name Fitz.

Morrigan: —I miss you. I miss you a thousand times over and then some. I miss you like the sun misses the moon on a constant basis because they never shall meet except for a brief moment in the sky. It kills me how much I want you back in my life despite all the things my doctors tell me you do to me. What if they're wrong? What if we're normal and they're the ones who have something failing them, a condition of sorts where they don't want anyone else to be happy?—

I look the words over, reading them carefully because I'll never get to take them back. They almost don't seem like I wrote them, and so I backspace to get rid of everything, only leaving the first three words. Propping myself up against the headboard of my little country bed, I brush the leftover salty tears from my eyes so hard I think I'm going to bruise.

The digits that make up his phone number stare back at me, daring me to dial them hear his voice again. As if by some kind of coincidence, a message from a different sender pops up on the screen.

Unknown: —Do you want to talk about anything? I'm in the barn with Stormy. Maybe a ride would do you some good. -L—

The unknown number—clearly belonging to Levy thanks to the uppercase *L* at the end of the note—serves to remind me I don't deserve the way I feel about someone like him. I'm conflicted about going down to the stable. I want to see Stormy, but I don't want the shame of having to face Levy's calm and collected demeanor, especially since I don't seem to be able to react in the same way.

Morrigan: —I'm all right. Thanks. How did you even get my number?—

Levy: —You don't seem okay. And I got it from your father. I told him you were hiding in your room and wouldn't talk to anyone.—

Morrigan: —Well, that's not true. I'm talking to you, now aren't I?—

Levy: —Get out of that bedroom and come see your horse. She needs a couple of carrots, and she knows that you're the one who brings them to her.—

I stifle a laugh, the sound coming out more like a choking noise.

Morrigan: —If I'm honest, I'm hiding up here because I'm embarrassed. You said it yourself, never a dull moment.—

How is it that it is so much easier to admit something to someone over the phone or on a message, but in person, I take the extra steps necessary to hide any inkling of interest in him?

Levy: —If you don't come out, I'm coming in.—

A hot crimson rushes up my neck, a leftover sob congesting my throat until I spit it out with a cough. I'm not really sure of what to say at the moment, but he doesn't give me a choice. In the long moments it takes me to make a decision, he's banging on the bedroom door.

My eyes are red and swollen, my cheeks tearstained. I lock the door with a click.

"C'mon now, Mo, talk to me," he says through the door, his velvety-smooth voice muffed out by the thick wood.

"I told you I'm fine. There is nothing to talk about." I lean my shoulder into the doorframe.

"I know you well enough to know that isn't true."

"You don't really know me at all."

"I'd like to."

I'm suddenly a mix of hot and cold, torn between a cold response or melting altogether, like a frozen lake succumbing to an unseasonably hot day.

I can hear the shifted weight, one boot to the other, a creak in the wood of the walls, and a bit of a thud, indicating he's sitting right outside my door, and I do the same. I can almost picture it, sitting back to back, the old wood separating us.

Suddenly, I want to tell him everything. Start at the beginning and not finish until he understands me completely and has no reservations about the things I have done and the person I have been, or he runs for the hills and ends things before they begin. But I don't want to hold back. I want him to know me.

"It's just a quote," I say, fiddling with the bracelet around my wrist. "My tattoo, that is."

He doesn't say anything, but I can tell he's listening.

"It says 'Everything We Are,' " I tell him, but I get choked up at the words I've said so many times. "My best friend and I got matching, best-friend tattoos on our eighteenth birthdays."

I can almost hear it, the vibration and the buzz of the tattoo gun, lying on the table, facing Jessie in the somewhat questionable tattoo shop in downtown Detroit. She had her shirt up around her chest, revealing her abdomen, checking her new ink out in the full-length mirror while the artist worked on my identical piece.

"What made you decide on that?" Levy asks, bringing me back to the conversation.

"We had been friends our whole lives. Our families celebrated holidays and birthdays together. My parents got divorced; her mother died a few years back. Through it all, we stayed best friends, side by side. Through thick and thin. No matter what and because of everything we are—were, that is." Tears fill my eyes, and I take an audible breath, the kind that catches on the emotions stuck in my throat.

"Morrigan?" He murmurs my name.

"We had exactly one rule." I manage to get the words out with a shaking breath. "In a friendship where there were very few guidelines and we always supported the other, we had one rule. I promised I would never, ever fall for her brother. She knew. She knew what he was like, and she didn't warn me. Or maybe she did, in her own twisted kind of way."

My chest tightens because this is the part I struggle to get past when I run through the story for myself, quietly. This is the part where I'm certain everything that has happened is my fault, even when everyone tells me it's not. It's partly my fault—and when I say partly, I mean mostly—because I broke that promise.

"But you can't help who you fall for, right?" I say, wiping away tears he can't see.

"Mo." His words are so quiet I almost miss them. "Open the door, please."

I reach up and unlock the door, then turn the handle, but neither of us moves. It's just like the phone; it's always easier to say what you want to say when you're not looking at the person directly. He places his hand through the threshold, and I place my hand on his. We take a break in the heavy conversation, and his thumb travels across the edge of the band around my wrist.

"Morrigan," he whispers, and goose bumps cover my skin from his touch—his voice. "Your dad told us a few months ago that he was thinking about leaving the ranch because his daughter had an accident." His voice is uneven, uncharacteristic of him. His words are turbulent, like the aircraft I came in on. He's clearly unsure if he should continue the question he's trying to ask. "It wasn't an accident, was it?"

"I had something with Fitz, you know."

"I do know, and from the sounds of it, it wasn't something good." Levy's dark eyes cast downward at the strap adorning my wrist.

"It's complicated."

"It doesn't sound complicated, Morrigan. It sounds like he was abusive."

"He wasn't abusive, Levy. He just had a different way of showing his intentions. He only ever wanted what was best."

I shift downward, unsure and slow, pulling on Levy's hand until we're sitting face-to-face on the hardwood of the hallway, me on the side of the doorframe in the bedroom while Levy spreads his legs over the threshold. Tears sit on my lower lid, teetering on the edge like all my emotions, while Levy keeps his gaze on me. Slowly but surely, I turn my hand over in his, exposing the tie that holds my wristband together. His gaze lingers for a moment, evaluating exactly what it is I'm telling him without using my words. With his free hand he pulls the strings.

The strap falls open, leaving my scarred wrist visible, cool house air running over the pale skin. Levy runs a finger across the marks, still healing—not quite old, but not quite new either. Even though I am fully clothed, I feel entirely exposed. Taking off that one accessory leaves me more naked than the removal of any other article of clothing would.

"He's brainwashed you into believing that. I'm sure the doctors have told you the same thing. But me saying it over and over again isn't going to change anything. You have to realize it on your own. People who love you won't treat you like how Fitz did. They won't drive you to cover your scars with bracelets and wristbands and defenses. They'll want you to be you— mistakes and pain and baggage and all."

I bite the inside of my lip as I melt into the oceanic

depths of Levy's eyes.

"And when you want to tell me what happened, I want you to know I'm here to listen. I can only put together so many pieces before I need you to fill in the blanks."

"That's it," I confirm. "That's everything. That's been my last—eternity."

Levy places the bracelet back onto my skin, and for the first time in the last minute, I can breathe again.

Chapter 8

Six days under the Alabama sky fly past, the sun and the moon rising and falling over and over again in a dance where they're always just missing one another. Thankfully, Levy and I are more like stars, appearing at the same time and forming something special together underneath the layers of a clear night. On the news each night, we watch the firefighters battle flames in nearby counties, and during the days we work the horses, take city folks on trail rides to the barren creek, and I learn the deeper layers of the ranch—and Levy too. The following Sunday's church service goes by without a hitch, and I neglect to pass out in the middle of the service, but by the time we get back to the farm, it's pouring out, and my white blouse is almost entirely see-through. Levy's right—there really never can be a dull moment with me.

By the time I get changed and wring some of the water from my bones, Levy's texted me to say the farrier's come to shoe a number of the horses, including Stormy after we take her for a ride. I tuck my head inside my old gray hoodie and go to put on my sneakers, but they're sopping with rain, and besides that, something just doesn't feel right. A beige box peeks out from underneath my bed, and I remember the cowboy boots my father gave me when I first arrived, all new and shiny with pretty stitching.

After pulling the cardboard box from underneath my askew blanket, I open it up and pull out the footwear before sliding one socked foot at a time into the Countryman boots. I don't really want to get them dirty, but I think putting them on has just cemented my place at the ranch. The dust and dirt and wrinkles in the leather will only serve as reminders of my work and time with Stormy and Levy.

Levy: —I'm in the barn with Stormy. The rain's stopped.—

Levy: —Bring her a treat? She'll love you forever for it.—

Morrigan: —You can bring them to her too, you know.—

Levy: —I also usually bring her you, which is about a thousand times more interesting for me. Keeps me up at night.—

I stare at the words on my phone as if they're not even real. A minute passes by before I get another text from Levy.

Levy: —Come down to the barn, Mo. Stormy's ready to go.—

Morrigan: —Okay.—

Shoving my phone in my back pocket, I temporarily distract myself from the idea of texting Fitz by turning my imagination to Levy, pushing away the nagging feeling of not being good enough and replacing the thoughts with more positive ones. My psychiatrist would be proud. By the time I stroll through the open barn door, I'm feeling better, the ticklish scent of horses and hay and fresh bedding serving as a type of aromatherapy. Levy meets me at the cross-ties, Stormy chomping quietly on the bit and waiting next to the boy with the raven-colored hair.

He hands the split reins to me as I pick up a helmet hanging from a stall door.

"Dried off a little?" Levy asks, Stormy's feet clip-clopping against the cement floor as we head out into the cloudy afternoon.

"A little. I think you saved me, to be honest. I was seconds away from melting away into nothing."

He chuckles a response, holding on to the side of Stormy's bridle while silently waiting for me to place my foot in the stirrup to hop on. Admittedly, I'm a little nervous to get on the horse for the first time, but I don't want to let Levy know I'm scared. With a deep breath, I shove my boot into the leather and swing my leg over the mare's back, anticipating a moment where she might take off after not having had a rider on her for however long. Levy doesn't look all that surprised when she stands stock-still, and it hits me at that moment he's definitely already had her out today for a ride just to make sure I would be safe.

"You rode her, didn't you?" I ask, picking up the reins and adjusting them between my fingers. "You wanted to make sure she wasn't going to go nuts when I got on."

"Your father's request," Levy admits with a tip of his head and a small smile. "I was going to throw you to the wolves, but he reminded me I should probably keep you all in one piece."

I give Stormy a little squeeze with my calves, and she moves off my leg and forward down the drive, Levy following next to the horse's head just in case.

"One piece would be nice." I pull my phone from my back pocket. "I'd also like to keep this in one piece so I can message you later. You know, keeping you up all night and all."

I pass the device down to Levy, who pockets the pink case and all in one smooth motion.

"I'm fine with it. I think you're fine with the idea too, judging by the blush on your cheeks."

"Maybe. I don't know. It's kind of hard." I shrug, my body shifting along with Stormy's cautious strides toward the back arena. She moves a little different than Rosie, shorter steps maybe, but with careful movements as if she knows somehow that she's carrying someone with no idea of what they're getting themselves into. "I almost texted him last night."

Levy gently pulls Stormy to a halt outside the gate, his brow furrowed as he looks up at the darkening sky. Words come ladling out of my mouth like alphabet stew, letters and sentences all jumbled together in a mess of confessions.

"I tried to commit suicide," I blurt, toying with Stormy's mane as we stand there outside of the riding ring. "Fitz got taken away by the police for hitting me at the front door one night, and my mother finally saw what he had done. I think by that time he'd hit me so many times I'd almost become immune to the beating, you know? But that time, it struck me differently. He was really angry with me for a conversation I'd had with a group partner. A guy. He was always jealous of other guys."

Levy leans against the fence post, petting Stormy's face and listening.

"I kind of fell apart when the cops showed up. I was bleeding and bruised, but I remember screaming his name as the officers put him in the car in handcuffs.

I didn't want him to go. I'd have probably let him hit me again if it meant he could have stayed."

Stormy lets out a heave of a sigh just then as if she understands the tale I'm telling and how it leads to the way I am today. I loosen the reins until I'm barely holding them, large loops forming in the leather. I wrap the ends around the horn of the saddle to secure them.

"Everything else is kind of a blur after that. I locked myself in the bathroom and just cut, over and over and over. I wanted desperately for anything to take me away. I wanted to be with Fitz; I wanted to vomit myself inside out for being such a willing victim to his violence. My heart and my head argued with each other so loud I couldn't even stand listening to the voices."

The wind starts to whistle, a heavy cloud rolling in over the bank of Colbourn Creek to our right. With one hand I unwrap the magnetized bracelet from around my wrist and roll my arm over to expose the scarred nature of my skin. The cuts still look fresh from my constant obsession with their existence, my fingers picking at the flesh over and over until it bleeds in long lines. However, I was able to leave them alone for the past week on the ranch, my mind mainly distracted by Stormy and Levy and the impending forest fires. I almost forgot they exist, except for brief moments in the shower where I scrub my hair and realize I have tendrils of Fitz's memory cascading down my arm.

Levy walks toward me, slowly, reaching up to take my hand in his own, and brushes his thumb over the marks he touched so tenderly only a few days ago. My skin sizzles with his touch, little shoots of fireworks exploding from everywhere he rubs his fingers.

"You didn't deserve this. I hope you know that."

"I want to know that," I reply, my voice so low and quiet I suspect we can both hardly hear it. "But still somehow I think I must have done something."

"For people like that, Mo, you don't have to have done anything. If it wasn't you, it could have been someone else. I feel like you weren't special, given the circumstances."

"Maybe," I murmur with a deliberate sigh.

"Not maybe." Levy releases my arm from his grasp. "Definitely not maybe."

The spell between us is broken by the sonorous rumble of thunder in the distance, rolling up and off the landscape to echo through the creek bed. Stormy pricks her ears toward the sound but doesn't even take a half-step sideways, the noise clearly not fazing her or her quiet nature. It's funny to think about, a little, that this is the same horse that had a mental breakdown when she came off the trailer just over a week before. Her prancing footsteps have been replaced with a solid kind of silence, reminding me of Levy, caring and kind and careful.

"Do you think it's still safe to ride?" I ask, looking overhead at the gathering smoke and cloud. Levy looks too, but I know he's reading the sky in a much different way than I'm able.

"I give it maybe five minutes before it starts pouring. Just enough time to walk her back down the driveway and say a little church-sanctioned prayer to the Lord for the rain showers." Levy gives me a little wink and turns Stormy back toward the barn. The mare follows along behind him, barely giving me any notice. Her pace picks up a little, the horse knowing she's heading back home.

We amble along the fence line in silence, a comfortable emptiness that surrounds us. I've come to realize that quiet is Levy's natural state of being, and I'm more than happy to sit in his company and simply be understood. However, we're only a couple of strides from the barn door when he speaks again, interrupting the steady sound of Stormy's hooves on the dirt and gravel.

"I'm glad you didn't text Fitz the other night." His voice is soft, dragging the sentence out over a few footfalls in order to make the words last. "I wish you didn't have his number, but I'm glad you were able to make yourself stop. What would you have told him anyway?"

A raindrop hits my hand as I sit there up on Stormy's back—my horse's back—thinking of what I'd really have liked to say in that message. "That I miss him. And I hurt every single day. But that I've found someone else, and I don't think I need him anymore."

"Why not?"

"Why would I? I have all this."

Just as the last words come out of my mouth, the downpour starts again, gray clouds opening into sheets of rain that crack across the Alabama sky.

Chapter 9

Sometime shortly after the rain begins, we spend a couple of hours in the barn, and I learn the finer points of shoeing horses before Hal Johnson drives back out to the road, leaving us alone under the noisy tin roof. Stormy munches a pile of hay in her stall as Levy tops up her water bucket. I sit on a plastic chair outside of the row of stalls, watching the rivers of rain pour down over Tin Star, wrapping my bracelet carefully back around my wrist to hide my own self-inflicted streams.

Needing someone is a difficult business, and I find once I get the words out of my mouth, I require that Levy say something to validate my feelings. Unfortunately for me, just as he goes to speak, the sky also decides to open up even more than I thought possible, rain falling in heavy sheets across the ranch. The sound of the weather pounds over top of the roofs and smashes into the dirt driveway, little speckles of water turning quickly into puddles and soaking the landscape. It creates a particular ambiance over our states of being—or at least mine, at a minimum—and makes me wonder if this is what real love is supposed to be. I can't quite tell.

Levy takes a seat across the aisle from me. "At least the rain will help the firefighters." He stretches his legs out across the corridor and looks toward the house. "Might have just saved us a lot of trouble. Most of them were contained, but a smaller one broke out up in Lafayette a couple of days ago. Little too close for comfort." He must be trying to make small talk, something I've yet to see him do.

I just nod, clasping the magnetic snap of my jewelry, before I redirect the conversation. I can't just leave my heart poured out all over this ranch and not get a response. "Levy?"

"Hmm?" he whispers, the sound so low it could be mistaken for a rumble of thunder.

"What are we doing?"

He sighs. "I don't know, Morrigan. But here's something I do know the answer to. You're wonderful. And I want us to be wonderful together. But I also don't want your father to kill me for touching you."

I laugh for what feels like the first time all day, and very well might be. "I'm not sure I agree that's a valid concern. I feel like he's been pushing us to spend time together ever since I arrived. I can't help but wonder if it's because he doesn't know what to do with me. I mean, my mother basically shipped me off here after telling him I tried to commit suicide. How would a parent even begin to know how to deal with that when I don't even know myself?"

"I'm not sure you're giving your father enough credit, Mo." Levy brushes his hair from his face. "I think he's been trying to process this whole thing since your grand appearance in Alabama. But it's hard because you won't exactly let him in on what's going on either. I mean you've already told me you're into me, and even I had to basically drag the words out of you."

Levy has a point because I haven't exactly been

forthcoming with any information; I recognize that now.

"I can't say I blame you, though," he adds, standing from his own plastic chair to lean in the doorway and watch the rain. "I don't imagine letting that confession out was easy for you."

A thunderhead rolls across the front field, dark and gray with misty edges. It's moving quickly, the rain not letting up even a tiny bit. Looking off across the pastures, I see a few spots of horses gathered under the trees and in the shelters, but more often than not they're still standing out in the paddocks munching away at the dried-out grass. Water falls off their bellies and hindquarters, dripping off manes and tails with exaggerated swishes, the occasional stomp from the ticklish nature of things accenting the casual allure of the afternoon. It's as if the rain changes nothing for the horses, and maybe it shouldn't change anything for us either.

"I'm going to go up to the loft and drop some more hay bales. You want to help? I always find work conducive to conversation." Levy turns toward my spot in the white plastic chair, nodding his head to one side.

"Do you think I'm broken?" I ask the question almost sparingly, the words hitching in my throat as they wait for a response. My skin on my wrist still sears with the feeling of his earlier touch.

"Oh, Morrigan." Levy sighs, scuffing one boot against a little pile of dust. "There's no right answer to that question."

He's right, again. There really isn't.

"You don't seem bothered by my past. This is the part where most people exit. Even people I had been friends with my whole life."

"We all have parts of our past that made sense to us at the time, but other people can't seem to figure out the reasoning for." He looks at the toes of his boots, and his voice travels across the barn in a distant fashion. It's as if he wanted to say it but maybe didn't mean for me to hear.

"You sound like you're speaking from experience," I prod, but the conversation pauses, the sound of the rain takes over, and we sit and listen to the patter of heavy rains.

I look down to twist the band on my wrist, and once I look up, he's staring my direction.

My phone pings, and I check it. The text from Dad is of the just-checking-in nature. I smile at the screen before sliding it in my back pocket. "Apparently he's worried about me being out here in the storm."

"Maybe he's worried about you being out here *with me* in the storm. You're his only daughter. We've been gone for hours. Dads tend to frown upon that."

He reaches a hand out, his fingertips skating across my hand, then he pulls away like he's thought better of it. My stomach clenches, and a new heat appears at my cheeks. My breath catches in my chest as my heart rate speeds up. I don't understand any of it, and for one moment, I almost think I'm dizzy, or stood up too fast, and then clarity comes over me. I more than just *like* him.

A smile crosses my lips, and he notices.

"What?" he says, a contagious smile growing over his teeth too.

"Nothing." *Everything*, I mean.

I tuck a piece of hair behind my ear, and when my

hand falls to my side, he catches it, and I let him lead me up to the hayloft.

The air is wet and humid with rain, the heat of the afternoon having risen up into the top of the barn and catching there due to the insulation of the bales. We toss a number of the big squares of hay down the chute to the corridor, baler's twine cutting into my fingers as I lift the heavy bundles. By the time we're finished, there's a fine sheen of perspiration on the back of my neck, and Levy's muscles are taut against the sleeves of his shirt. He lifts the hem of his shirt with a smirk, using the fabric to wipe at his face, exposing chiseled stomach muscles and tanned, narrow hips.

I've never seen a boy in real life with a body like that, and then it strikes me that perhaps I've never really seen a man like this at all.

I collapse in a tired heap onto one of the large nearby hay bales, and Levy takes refuge next to me. He lies on his back, the same way I do, and his head tilts until his eyes find mine. The symptoms return full force, the increased heart rate, the sweat beads at the back of my neck. He might kiss me, and I might let him. He leans in, and I take a deep breath. I lean in to meet him, but he pulls away.

The heat that floods my cheeks is not that of a young crush but embarrassment. Apparently, I read him all wrong, and now I don't know what to do or say. "Oh, I'm s-sorry?" The words come out as a question.

"No, Mo, it's not like that."

I'm already stepping away from him, distractedly brushing hay from my jeans. I don't know what to do about the situation except get out of there as fast as possible, my mind racing over and over and over for me to leave, escape.

I scoot my way down the ladder before taking off into the rain.

"Mo!"

Levy's call cuts through the storm. An urgency is in his voice, one that calls me back, but I resist the feeling and simply stop, the rain soaking my hair and clothes. He approaches from behind, his own boots crackling along the gravel, and places his hands at my hips, but I don't turn around. The puddles all around us ripple from new raindrops, and neither of us move. We stand there, getting wet, doing nothing and something all at the same time.

"It's not that I don't want to kiss you," he says as if he's reading my mind.

"What is it, then?" I turn to face him.

"I just wanted to make sure you're ready." His eyes are genuine, the meaning behind his words as heavy as the rain.

"Oh," I say, quiet. I'm not used to a guy being patient or kind. I didn't know what it looked like until now.

"I like you, Mo. I think you're wonderful. But the last guy you were with, he made all your decisions for you. This time, I want all the decisions to be yours. So when you're ready, I will be too. I'm giving you the reins, so to speak." He smiles and pulls me close.

I nod, a drop of water dripping off my nose.

"Come on. I'll walk you to the house."

We walk a slow, drawn-out path back to the house, despite the wet weather. As we near the porch, I find myself wishing we weren't. The walk is quiet, calming, cleansing. We reach the porch, and I take the first two steps, leaning into the railing under the cover of the porch roof.

Levy places one boot on the first step and leans into the same railing. "Until tomorrow, then." He tilts his hat.

"Until tomorrow," I whisper back, unsure what to say but finding myself not wanting him to leave. He turns on his heel and heads toward the truck. I can't help but watch as he walks away, his sculpted muscles protruding against his rain-slicked clothes with every step he takes.

I think back to us sitting on the floor in my room, his face calm as he ran his fingers against the self-inflicted wounds on my arms, the barn, where I thought he would kiss me and didn't, and then what he said— the reins are in my hands. He *gets* me. He's wonderful, calm, patient. And then for the first time in I'm not sure how long, I want to do something exciting and unscripted and spontaneous. Something that scares me but frees me too.

"Levy!" I call through the rain, and he stops, turning to face me. I step down from the porch and walk quickly, a skip almost, toward him.

The sky opens up and pours even harder, if that's even possible. I can barely see through the rain as I break into a run and take off toward Levy, boots stomping through makeshift puddles on the driveway. His smiling silhouette waits for me, and he steps away from the open truck door, seemingly thinking that maybe I have one more thing I'd like to say. Instead, I crash into his chest, putting my hands at his neck, and pull him down to meet me in the kiss I've been waiting weeks for. Every nerve in my body starts to unravel, releasing the tension I've been carrying around for months, passing it through my lips into his mouth with fervor. He seems surprised at first, maybe just for a split second, then he too falls into the embrace, his tongue touching my mouth as he deepens the kiss into everything I've ever wanted.

It lasts forever and not long enough.

"Goodnight," I whisper against his lips.

His fingers thread through my belt loops.

He gives me a wink before releasing me back into the rain. I crash through the front door in something of a waterfall, soaked through to the bone and then some, the screen slamming behind me with a squeal.

My father is in the kitchen, somewhere I swear he never leaves. "How are you feeling, Morrigan? Levy show you anything?" He pours a steaming cup of coffee into a patterned mug and pushes it toward me as I kick off my boots.

"Got a little walk on Stormy before the rain hit. Better than nothing."

My father nods, staring out the bay window at the flat hills, an absent gesture if nothing else. "Good the rain's come in, though. Will help the firefighters." There's a pause just then before he continues with a different topic. "By the way, I found some old horse books in the basement crawl space when I was looking for my old work shirts for rags. I've left them on your bed. Today's a good day for reading if I've ever seen one."

The mention of my bedroom and a distraction sounds like the perfect way to get myself out of having a conversation right now, my lips likely still chapped and crimson from Levy's mouth over them.

"I'm going to get changed, and then I'll check them out. I think I need to take it easy for the rest of the day. My head's a little woozy," I lie. Dad doesn't seem to notice. He goes to open his mouth to respond, but before he gets the opportunity, crackling white light streaks across the sky, followed by a sonorous bang, the window panes rattling with the noise. I must jump half a foot in the air, spilling hot coffee all over the floor of the kitchen in spattered droplets.

"Christ!" I curse, using the Lord's name in vain in such a way that I know it would be frowned upon in the Creek. "Is that thunder?"

"Sounds like we're finally getting a big one." He tosses me a dishrag from atop the counter. I swipe at the burning parts of my skin to remove the beads of coffee while he uses another towel to sweep up the tile.

"I'd say."

"Don't you worry about it." Dad smiles knowingly, perhaps after all this time remembering the magic I see in thundershowers. "You go take a rest down in your room, and I'll have supper ready in an hour or so. We can eat on the wooden swing outside. Under the overhang is the best place to watch the light show. It's not going to end any time soon."

He drops both cloths in the sink and sprays them with the nozzle until they're sopping wet, while I take my coffee and pad down the hallway in my hay-covered socks, leaving a little trail of debris and secret memories on the wooden floor.

Chapter 10

My father and I watch the blazing lights until well after dark, rain flooding the pastures into lakes and gathering the outdoor horses in their respective shelters. The stormy weather doesn't let up, Dad long since retired to bed in order to rise early, and it's far past midnight when I finally head back to my room after washing up the dinner plates as quietly as possible. Because I'm feeling nostalgic from the outdoors, the hayloft, and everything else during the day, I send Levy a little goodnight text with the selfish hope that he'll be awake to answer it. I snap a picture of the lightning over the ranch, a perfectly timed snapshot of an ultraviolet purple streak that leaves the heavens and touches the earth, illuminating everything in its path, only for half a second. Underneath it, I write *wish you were here*.

When I don't hear anything after five minutes, I peel off my clothes and dump them on the bedside chair before crawling underneath the quilt. As is a tradition with the things that I do, I catch myself browsing through Fitz's degrading texts before rolling over, listening to the pitter-pattering on the roof and the wall as the rain falls sideways against it.

I don't know why I do it—look at those texts, I mean—but I continue to as if the words are somehow both killing me and keeping me alive.

At some point, I pass out with my phone in my hand. I only know this because when there's a rap on my window a couple of hours later, I drop the screen right on my face.

"What the actual hell?" The words come out of my mouth in a hushed whisper, meant to communicate to nobody in particular. I wait amid the sound of the rain warring against the window until there's a rapping sound again. It's then, and only then, I see the outline of a person standing there, rain soaking through their clothing. My heart skips a beat as I wonder who could be outside on a night and at a time like this. Instinct tells me it's someone trying to break into the house, but lightning illuminates the sky, showing the clear silhouette of Levy standing at my window.

I crack the window and whisper into the wet air. "Are you *crazy*?"

"You said you wished I was here. Wish granted." He's barely audible over the rain.

"Go to the side door. Just try not to make any noise. My father will kill us both if he knows I'm sneaking you into this bedroom."

I quickly dress in what is likely a mismatched pile of clothes from the bedside chair. The mountain has grown bigger over the past week or so, due to me having neglected to do my laundry in favor of caring for Stormy and doing barn chores. I find the items that smell least like a horse—a pale yellow tank top and a pair of blue fabric shorts—and creak open the bedroom door to listen for any noise of my father being awake. I hold my breath and count to ten inside my head before tiptoeing over to the side door where Levy's shadow waits.

"You scared the crap out of me," I whisper under my breath. "Get in here."

"Gladly."

He wrings out his hair under the canopy of the side porch before kicking off his boots and stepping inside. I place a finger to my lips in a vague attempt to tell him to be quiet as I guide him around the corner to my bedroom, as if he doesn't already know where it is. Making a tiny detour, I grab a pile of towels from the bathroom closet, then once the door is closed, we speak in hushed tones.

"I couldn't not see you tonight," he starts, dripping all over the floor of the room with his soaked T-shirt and jeans.

I unfold a towel and hand it to him before plunking myself down on the bed. "You're going to make yourself sick standing out in the rain like that. What am I supposed to do with a wet stable hand in my bedroom? It's not like I have any clothes to give you."

He rubs himself all over with the bath sheet, rain still dripping from his raven hair in the moonlight. "I could take them off," he says in a slow, quiet voice that slips right under my skin and leaves goose bumps head to toe. I nearly choke on my own saliva, Levy's words getting caught in my mind. He's smiling from across the room, and I know he's said it just to get a rise out of me, and it's worked. "Easy, Mo. I'm kidding. I just came over to talk."

"We could have texted if you wanted to talk," I remind him, patting the spot on the bed where my phone has slipped down to.

He pulls an elastic band from his wrist and snaps it into place around his hair, making a perfectly small bun before taking the towel, squeezing the excess water from the style, and taking a seat at the edge of my bed. "You're trying to make it sound like you don't want me here, but I know you do. You wouldn't have let me in otherwise, and you wouldn't have kissed me this afternoon." There's a pause, the night dripping in and our faces drawing closer. "Do you believe in love at first sight, Morrigan?" His voice hangs heavy and warm in the bedroom air.

The question might be a rhetorical one, but I feel compelled to answer because I think I gave a shit answer the first time he asked me the question.

"I used to," I reply softly, a whispered lilt to my voice that matches his own. "You know, before." I tuck a loose strand of hair behind my ear.

"That's interesting." He clasps his hands together and rests them between his thighs. His eyes tell me that isn't the answer he wanted. "You stopped believing in love at first sight when I finally started."

The words come along with a rumble of thunder, Levy's voice trailing off as his dark eyes find mine. I'm staring directly into his soul when something hits me—I had stopped believing in a lot of things. I don't know what to say because everything he's said is true—again. So instead, I just sit there like an idiot, staring at him, watching his clothing stick to him in all the right places.

"I don't want to hurt you, Morrigan," he murmurs. "I don't want to make you feel the things Fitz did. But in about three seconds I'm going to kiss you, and you're going to get wet from all this fabric, and then you're going to have to decide if I'm allowed to keep going."

I want him to kiss me, and I want him to keep

going. Not because I think it will erase a part of Fitz that has ruined me, but because I think I'm genuinely crazy about Levy, and I haven't been able to get him off my mind. Thankfully for me and my wild heart, he pulls me in close to him, so close I can feel his heart beating hard against the dampness of his black shirt and smell the scent of outdoors and maybe a little bourbon. He's not drunk. It's more like an afterthought, an after-smell.

"You're not going to hurt me, Levy. I don't think you're capable of it."

"Oh, I could, Mo. I've hurt beautiful women before when I was younger. But I don't ever want to again."

"When you were younger?" I grin into his broad chest. "You're barely old."

He fingers the hem of my tank top before letting his warm hands slide underneath the fabric to rest on my skin. Little pulsations of electricity bounce between us, and outside, like maybe we are the weather and we've brought the storm indoors. I am lightning, and he is thunder, and together we make the music of lifted Alabama drought and prisms of multi-colored rainbows.

"Maybe I'm an old soul."

"Maybe I like that about you."

"We're falling into a history of a lot of maybes," he mumbles, tipping my chin toward his lips, the bourbon smell lingering and making me drunk by association.

"Maybe we are."

Our lips touch, briefly, then we explode into the caverns of the night, all hands and mouths and bodies pressing backward onto the sheets. He pulls off his wet shirt and tosses it onto the floor. My hands find their way all over his upper body, feeling the muscle built from lifting hay and training horses, his tanned skin rippling in the blackness of the bedroom and accented by the occasional bolt of naked lightning that has yet to wane. Thunder rolls, but I can't tell anymore if it's in my head or somewhere deep in the pit of my stomach, an angry grumble of the sky or my body's impatience in waiting to have the rest of Levy.

"Are you sure about this, Mo?" he whispers into my neck, licking the soft spot underneath my ear as I dig my nails into his shoulder blades. One hand has fingers wrapped in what they can of my hair, the other holding his body above me, hovering, whispering against my own bare skin.

"I'm sure."

He bites his lip as he gazes at me like I'm the only girl he's ever seen like this, a little, vulnerable heart so carefully placed in his large hands, totally absorbing the magnitude of the early Alabama air, feeling the ways in which I want him.

"You'll tell me if you change your mind?"

"I don't plan on changing my mind, cowboy."

A soft chuckle escapes from somewhere deep in his throat, a warm sound that calms my pattering heart into a steady rhythm.

"I'm serious, Levy. I want this."

That's all the confirmation he needs because after those words, we don't stop until the thunder picks up again, banging on the walls of the house to remind us we're very much alive.

We're lying there later, wrapped up in each other and warmth and knotted sheets, when the lightning starts again. It's closer this time, sizzling and crackling as it hits somewhere over near Alamo City in the woods and in the empty fields of the northwest side of the property. The rain teems down in such a way that it makes the weather from earlier look like a dry mist, and I think I could scream out and my father wouldn't even hear the sound of my voice. This is probably for the best because I know for a fact that Levy and I weren't exactly silent in our endeavors.

"It's closer, I think," I note, adjusting my head on Levy's bare shoulder. "Sounds louder than earlier."

"It's pretty much overhead now. I think we're in the worst of it."

There's nothing between us but a thin blanket and the wrap around my wrist, and I've never felt more at home than I do in this very moment, here with him in a bubble of our own kind of perfection. As I realize it, he shifts the sheet between his legs, crinkling it so our skin touches, and brushes his fingertips against the wristband I'm wearing.

"How many of these do you have?" he asks, keeping the peace between the sheets. "I feel like I've seen a few of them repeated now."

"Five or six." I think about all the bracelets and whatnot stashed away in my dresser drawer now that I've unpacked my things in a little more detail. "I guess I didn't want to make it too obvious I was wearing it for a reason."

"You know, you don't have to hide from us here at Tin Star, Morrigan. You're not the first broken soul we've seen, nor will you be the last."

"I know. I believe you. I just, I don't know. Maybe I'm not ready."

He snorts, the sound almost entirely hidden by a

particularly loud rumble of thunder. "And you were ready for all this? You're stronger than you think you are, *uwoduhi*."

I almost don't catch that the last word isn't English, but it slips out of his mouth so carefully and gently I know it can't be.

"*Uwoduhi*. What does that mean?" I butcher the pronunciation because I can't get my tongue to wrap around the letters the way he can.

"It's Cherokee."

"For what?" I poke him in the side, and he wriggles away, rolling over on top of the sheet and uncovering my now-bare legs. "Probably an insult that I'll never understand. It will be five years from now, and you'll still be calling me *uwoduhi*, and I'll be over here thinking it means 'precious strawberry' and it actually means 'brazen psychopath.' "

"You're thinking about five years from now?" He raises an eyebrow, and I swear there's a twinkle in his eye.

"Don't change the subject," I prod. "What's *uwoduhi* mean?"

"It means beautiful."

There's a pregnant pause filled with a flash of light from outside before I respond. "Oh."

Suddenly, Fitz's saved messages start running through my head. I don't have to look at them to know what they say in my inbox. I have them memorized after reviewing them every night before bed.

Fitz: —You're beautiful, Morrigan, but you're not all that bright sometimes.—

Fitz: —I love you, beautiful.—

Fitz: —You'd be more beautiful without those

bruises you make me give you. I wouldn't hit you if you didn't deserve it.—

"It's a compliment, Mo." Levy interrupts my thoughts, and I realize I'm chewing on the inside of my cheek. I can tell by his tone he knows something's not quite right. "Did I say something wrong?"

"N-no," I start, stammering over the letters. "I was just thinking, is all. Last person to say anything like that to me was Fitz. But he always had a way of giving it an aggressive undertone."

"What do you mean?" He closes his arms around me, keeping me warm and safe feeling amid the torrential rain shower. "I think I need an example."

I shake my head as best as I can from my horizontal position. "Never mind, I shouldn't have said anything. What other Cherokee words do you know?"

"*Vtla*, Morrigan. Tell me about Fitz."

I take a deep breath and let out a long sigh before rolling over to grab for my phone, stuffed well underneath a mass of pillows at the head of the bed. I poke at the home button and navigate to the messages app where I click on Fitz's name.

"I've saved all his messages, Levy. I can't get rid of them. And every time I feel bad about myself or too good about my life, I seem to have this compulsion to go back and read them and remind myself that maybe Fitz was the best thing I'll ever get. That maybe I don't deserve anything better than him."

Levy carefully takes the phone from between my fingers, scrolling up and up and up through the text bubbles. He slides himself against the headboard, back pressed on the wood, and stares at the device for a long time, reading the blue and gray messages in his head. I curl my body into the gap created by his left arm, pulling the blue sheet over my chest, breathing in that familiar bourbon scent and not wanting to let it go.

"I almost can't believe these are real," he notes after a while.

I've counted three lightning strikes by the time he talks, and one seems scarily close to the barn, but I'm sure it's just a trick of my imagination.

"Morrigan, didn't the doctors tell you to get rid of these?"

"They did, but—I don't know. I guess I don't know. I feel like he's part of me now, forever. He was my first. My first of a lot of things."

"He should be the last of probably almost all those things too, from what you've told me."

"Maybe."

"This isn't a maybe situation. This isn't healthy, Mo. You really should delete his number from your phone and get rid of all these notes. They're dangerous."

My eyes start to well up with tears as I think about deleting Fitz from my life. I remember screaming on the sidewalk when the police took him away. I remember the times when he was nice to me, and the times he wasn't. I remember all too many things and forgive much too easily. It is that moment I know Levy is right, and Fitz's memory in my phone is only going to keep destroying me night after night, and I really should get rid of him for good.

"I'd delete them, but..." I pause, looking up at Levy's dark eyes with a tightness in my chest. "I just can't. I can't bring myself to do it."

"Can I delete them?" He uses the question as

gently as possible. "Maybe this is something you need a little bit of help with. I don't want to push you too hard, but I think maybe with this you need someone you trust telling you to let go."

"It's only been a few weeks."

"What is time, Morrigan, but a construct? Something to tell us when to forage and fight and fu— well, you know. Does it tell us when the right time to fall in love is? How many times we need to see each other before everything's gonna be all right? Our hearts tell us that, and we follow them to the ends of the earth. What's your heart telling you?"

I don't get to answer, because an urgent-sounding knock at my bedroom door scares the hell out of me.

"Morrigan, get up! The barn's on fire!"

Chapter 11

I stare at Levy's worried expression for a solid five seconds before I realize what my father's words mean, the magnitude of the statement hitting me square in the face. *The barn is on fire. The barn is on fire. The barn is on fire.*

Levy jumps into action before I even manage to process the words. Dad's facial expression is lost somewhere between worried about the flames and *we'll talk about this later.* There's no time to worry about what my dad is going to say about Levy and me spending the night together because that's a conversation for another time. A time when we aren't about to lose everything.

"Did you call the fire department?"

Levy's voice is strong and clear, his silhouette making a broad shadow in the darkness of the hallway. The response is muffled, he and my father clambering down the hallway and out the side door with a slam. I'm half tripping over my own feet as I shove my legs into my shorts while running down the corridor, the dread and anxiety I was already feeling over Levy's anger about my past intensified by the news of the fire. As I open the storm door, pushing my tank top down over my stomach, I spot Levy and Dad running across the driveway for the barn. Gravel and water kick up from their feet and patter away.

The early morning is dark and still, but angry red flames spew from the rooftop of the building, thick plumes of acrid smoke billowing out into the raging thunder and lightning storm as if it might put out the fire in the sky. Haunting screams of horses banging to get out of their stalls echo into the night, crackling tendrils scooping out from the hayloft where Levy and I had almost shared our first kiss.

I run after the two of them, but I'm groggy. By the time I catch up to Levy, my father's diving through the front door of the stable and disappearing into the burning building.

"We've got to go in and unlock the stalls and get the horses out before the loft falls on their heads. Your dad and I will pass them to you, and you get them in a pasture as fast as you can, two at a time."

"You're not going in there, are you?" I croak, coughing from the smoke and the dust. The heat is overwhelming even standing outside like I've been placed in a sauna with the temperature turned up way too high.

"We've got to get the horses; the fire department will be here any minute, but the horses might not have that kind of time. Be careful."

Levy doesn't wait for my response. I've already wasted precious seconds with my blathering, and he turns his back to me before falling into the barn after my father, who is already coming out the door with Rebel in tow, a towel wrapped over the horse's face. I can tell from the body language of the horse that he's petrified, but my father's work with the colt has paid off because he follows behind Dad carefully, halter half on his face.

Thunder crackles across the Alabama morning, shaking the very core of my existence and causing Rebel to shy away.

"Take him, quick!"

My father shoves the horse into my hands, pulling the towel off before I have a chance to think, and I break into a quick run across the driveway based purely on instinct. Rain pounds on my head and on Rebel's hindquarters, the animal quivering beside me. I practically launch him into the paddock near the house, leaving him to gallop off in the field away from the fire and the smoke. As I look up into the distance, Levy's coming from the burning barn, two horses in his hands. My legs can hardly carry me from one end of the property to the other fast enough, the gate of the paddock left swinging open.

"How many are inside?" I ask, breathless, as Levy takes a deep breath of the cleaner air.

His skin is red in the nighttime, fire flickering in his dark eyes. "Stalls are full. Maybe twenty. I unlocked all the doors, but the horses won't run. They don't feel safe. We've got to lead them out. Here." He has lead lines wrapped around Chance and Rosie's necks, the towel over Chance's eyes just like my father did with Rebel. "We're running out of time. We're gonna try to run them out into the driveway and pick 'em up later. Otherwise, we're going to lose them. Take these two and stay out of the way once the herd comes running."

At that moment, Dad breaks through the smoke with four horses, two mares and their babies following behind as if their lives depend on it. I guess they do.

"Take the ones with the leads, Mo! They'll all follow behind wherever they see Rosie going."

I don't think. I just do. I grab the woven cotton lead around Rosie's neck and take off in a run, the herd of horses released by Levy and my father frantically following along behind, whinnying. Puddles splash along our feet and hooves, and I whip the line off Rosie's neck once I get her in the paddock, throwing myself out of the way of the crash of horses running to safety. They follow after Rebel, who neighs from far over in the corner of the field, a crack of lightning resounding over their heads.

There's a crash in the distance, and even from my position across the driveway, I can see a portion of the barn roof collapse. Thick, black vapor flies from the new hole created in the building, the burning embers of the wood making the stable a gigantic cigarette. It's possible that I scream, but the sound is replaced by choking as I break across the homestead. Without thinking, without much of anything, I lurch through what's left of the front doorway and call through the fire.

"Building's coming down! We've got to hurry!" Smoke asphyxiates me, my eyes blinded by the mist and the fallen beams. My skin is burning, like I'm being microwaved on the outside, beads of sweat crawling over my face and getting stuck in my clothes.

"Dad! Levy!"

"Go around the side! We'll meet you there!" Levy's voice is weak, strangled, but audible.

I dart around the building to the side stable door where the structure has only just started smoking, little bits of fire falling from the ceiling and horses forcing their way out the door to the attached pasture. The rain has slowed now, not enough to dampen the barn any longer, and the fire rages along the front side out of control.

"Levy!"

Levy trots down the aisle with Stormy, towel over her eyes, and I breathe a sigh of relief at seeing the gray mare and the boy coming from the stable.

"We've gotten them all out from the other side, the side that collapsed." He pants, his long hair sticking to his face, having fallen from the bun it was tied into. He lets go of Stormy, and she gives me a cursory glance before taking off to join the other animals in the field. "Pull the leftover horses out from this wing and get them into the back pasture. Should be enough space between them and the barn. I'm going to find your dad."

He scrambles down the aisle way without another word, leaving me to pull open stall doors and lead two nervous horses at a time into the pasture up from the barn.

Once, when I was in elementary school in Michigan, I went to a fire department for a class trip. They had us all sit on the floor for a minute without doing anything, and then at the end, they told us that we have, on average, one minute to get out of a burning building. While, from my spot on the floor of the professional center, that one minute seemed to last forever, more than one minute has passed since we started clearing horses from the barn. We're rescuing on borrowed time, and now my father is still in there somewhere, Levy running to his potential rescue.

I can't do anything other than pull horse after scared horse from the barn until the stalls are empty and I can't breathe any longer. What feels like seconds turns into ten or twenty minutes before the Alamo City Fire Department rolls up the driveway with their sirens blaring, lights blinking all around and brightening up the morning sky with more red.

Red, everything is red.

I run toward the truck as if I'm going to be able to do something, while firefighters fall from the vehicle before some pull out yellow hoses and point them at the stable.

"My Dad and—" I don't know what to call Levy. "—one of the ranch hands are in there! Part of the roof collapsed while they were trying to get the horses out!"

One of them stops pulling the hose, surveying the area quickly. "Is there another door?"

"Around the side!" I yell, the noise of the sirens nearly drowning me out.

Two men in yellow uniforms, helmets sealed to their heads, rush around the side of the building and disappear into the fire with what looks like no fear at all. I watch in amazement as they run headlong into the burning barn, no hesitation or pause in their step, much like my father and Levy when they knew they had to get in there and save the horses. My heart aches for them, my brain scrambles in panic for what to do next, and my body freezes into a standing corpse with absolutely no use at all.

The next few minutes are a flurry of activity. One firefighter covers me in a blanket and sits me off to the side of the paddock, out of the way from the second truck that makes its way up the drive to unload more firefighters. Hoses uncoil, dragging like thick snakes along the roadway, water pouring on the precarious roof like forced waterfalls. Trusses turn black and sizzle as the liquid contains some of the fire, turning parts of what's left of Tin Star Ranch into a smoky, dark blister.

One firefighter slowly emerges from the rubble and flames, Levy leaning against his tall frame and weighing the man down on one side. He's coughing loudly, gasping for clean air, and his mouth is moving as if he's trying to talk, but I can't hear the words from my distance. I start to get up from my spot on the fence, but one of the firefighters stops me with one hand, and I instantly feel helpless and unnecessary.

"Better stay back, miss. Let us tend to the scene now. There's nothing more for you to do."

"But he's my—"

I'm talking to nobody because the firefighter doesn't wait for my response, instead busying himself with repositioning one of the yellow hoses that is mucky from the driveway. I don't know how to end that sentence anyway, so instead, I shut my mouth and watch the pieces of my father's pride and joy turn into scraps of nothing. My heart slams erratically in my chest, the heat of the night still coursing through my veins and making my hair feel as if it's burning up on the ends.

A little white ambulance finally wails up the road, skidding over the gravel before parking in the middle of the driveway. The sirens shut off abruptly, lights intermingling with those from the house and the fire trucks, and I watch as two people exit from either side and traipse their way to the fire chief for instructions. Some words are exchanged as I toy with the fringes of the gray blanket, the material itching my bare shoulders where I've been burned, and it takes everything in me not to run up to Levy and check him all over to make sure he's going to be all right.

Instead, I do as I'm told and impatiently watch the water spouts slowly weaken the fire into a few little tendrils while worrying about my father. I don't think my legs would carry me even if I wanted them to, but thankfully Levy gives me a little wink as he passes by to let me know everything's going to be okay. At least, I hope that's what it means.

I sneak past the firefighter who told me to stay and follow Levy to the back of the ambulance, where they have him sit on the edge of the bumper to breathe oxygen from a tank. Glancing back, I keep watching for the second firefighter out of the corner of my eye.

"Levy, Jesus Christ. You could have been killed."

"Your dad—" He gasps, the mask suctioned over his face.

"They'll get Dad," I reply, a bit of hesitation to my voice. Where is that damn firefighter anyway?

"No, Mo." Levy sucks in a deep breath of air, pausing to hack out half of one of his lungs. "He got caught under one of the collapsed beams. I tried to pull him out…"

Voices begin to tumble around the ranch, conversations muddling with the sights and sounds of a fire scene—pushing, neighing, dragging, crackling.

"Pearson, we need CPR! Get him in a bed and hook him up!"

"Radioed the hospital, let 'em know we're on our way."

Everything happens so quickly I barely have time to process it. The second firefighter, the one who has the lead on entering the barn, appears from the smoke and the rubble with a body toppled over his shoulder.

The morning light behind him casts an awkward shadow on the driveway, but I know in an instant my father isn't doing well since he'd never willingly let himself be carried anywhere. Other men rush to the firefighter's side, crowding Dad and rumbling a gurney down the gravel road as water flies overhead. The thunder and lightning have all died down now, but the sky is a thick blue and crimson, telling me based on the old folklore that the atmosphere is warning of more weather to come.

I turn to run toward my father, but Levy grabs my wrist and holds on.

"Let them work, Mo. We'll follow behind in my truck to Alamo City Regional."

Levy moves out of the way just fast enough to have the bed trundle to the edge of the ambulance, legs folding up to push into the back. Dad's covered in a sheet, only his face showing, one paramedic blowing air from some kind of hand pump into my father's mouth. His skin is red along his neck and face. Under the white blanket, I presume the worst.

"You need observation," one paramedic says to Levy as the other shuts one back door of the vehicle. "Police are meeting us at the hospital for you to provide statements for insurance. Hop in."

Levy shakes his head, gesturing to his truck at the side of the house as the firefighters turn off their hoses to our right, the barn dripping with water and foam. "We'll drive our way in." The words come out as pieces, broken in the spaces in between. As soon as Levy gets them out, another coughing fit hits, turning him a violent shade of red as he struggles to breathe. I want to help him—comfort him, offer him something—

but I'm frozen to the spot.

"You really should come with us," the medic says with a slightly chiding tone. "Smoke inhalation is a dangerous thing. You don't want to risk it."

"I'm—I'm not leaving Morrigan." Then more coughing.

"Son, we have to go now. We have to get this man to the hospital. Last chance." The paramedic looks at me as if maybe I'll be able to talk some sense into Levy.

I guess maybe I can. Kneeling, I place my hand on Levy's cheek, his skin hot with fatigue and the heat of the flames that licked at the barn walls. "Just go, Levy," I plead, my voice hoarse from the smoke. "I'll be right behind you. We need a car there. I'll take Dad's truck."

"You're sure?" His eyes are filled with worry. He—who ran into a burning building, risked his life trying to save the horses and my father, hasn't properly inhaled in too many minutes—and he's still more worried about me than himself.

"I promise." I stroke his hair back behind his ear in a gesture that almost seems like it doesn't belong to me. "Go."

The words taste like a campfire.

Levy goes, shuffling his way into the back of the ambulance while I try and will my eyes to suck back up the tears doing their best to sneak out. If he sees me crying, there's no way he'll stay in that van. Thankfully, I'm able to hold myself together until the man shuts the other door to the ambulance, flipping on some switch to start the sirens wailing. Once again, everything is red and noisy. I stand and stare as the white van turns in a loop before quickly and carefully speeding down the bumpy driveway. Once it disappears around the corner, I'm finally able to breathe and try to convince myself the worst part of the night is over now. They're going to take the best care of my father and Levy. They're going to hook Dad up to some machines and treat his skin.

Everything's going to be all right.

Chapter 12

Breaking into a sprint, I run as fast as my legs will allow. My boots kick up mud and puddles as I take off down the driveway toward the log house, and I launch myself through the front door without removing my boots. Unlike most regular people, Dad doesn't keep his keys by the entryway or even on a key hook, but rather in the makeshift office he uses for ranch paperwork and taxes, the few times a year he actually gets around to doing either. Unfortunately, as I dig through the stacks of books, papers, and forms, I find no obvious keys anywhere. As I rip open the top drawer of the desk, a small bin of paper clips falls to the floor, raining around me like metal confetti. There, sitting on top of a smooth handgun case, are the truck keys.

After crashing out the front of the house, I gallop across the driveway and clamber into the truck while kicking debris all over the floor mats. The scent of pine and sandalwood hits me the second I open the door, and as I shove the key into the ignition, I spot a new air freshener hanging from the rearview mirror. The truck starts with a roar, country radio station blasting ten decibels too loud. I punch the radio button so I have silence and whip the steering wheel around to turn out of the drive and past the post-and-rail pastures.

Intent on driving to the hospital in record time, I cruise over the traffic-less highway ten miles above the posted limit, the double yellow line flowing past like the hoses used to put out the fire. Warm air rushes in on a breeze, and the scent of smoke, air freshener, and mud get temporarily washed away. While I appreciate that my speed is some kind of vague attempt to catch up with the ambulance and not miss a second of my father's diagnosis, the soundtrack of Levy's persistent hacking concerns me in a different way. My father is strong—he's always been. A barn fire won't be the thing to take him out.

The Alamo City Regional more closely matches a shopping mall than a hospital. It is smaller than the familiar hospital in Michigan I was always in and out of, maybe five floors maximum, with a brick front, and a row of benches along a tree-lined plaza. Atop the flat roof, the sun rises, all bright and yellow and reflecting off the puddles in the lot as if the violent night at the ranch didn't happen.

As I twist the key to the off position in the ignition, it's only then I realize I'm holding my breath. I haven't been in a hospital since my release following the suicide attempt, and I begged my doctor on multiple occasions not to bother sending me home. I still, even after all that, didn't want to live without Fitz in my life. Now I'm struggling to exist in a world where I know he's still around.

"I-I don't think I can do this," I say to nobody, my voice shaking with the syllables as my quivering hands ball up into tight fists in my lap. "I haven't been inside a hospital since…"

My voice trails off, the word *suicide* like arsenic on my lips. If I say it, it will find a way to get to me. However, if I leave the term dangling in the wilderness of time and space, then it's almost as if it was never really there, reminding me life isn't like what it used to be in Michigan. Alabama is a whole other world away, the city lights of downtown traded in for a full dark, starry nights, and boys like Fitz exchanged for people like Levy who understand that wild hearts and quiet afterthoughts can equal something extraordinary. It makes me think that maybe, in some corner of my mind, I'll stay here in Colbourn Creek forever and help figure out what to do with what's left of Tin Star Ranch.

Poking the key back into the ignition, I turn it halfway so the radio blinks on. An old song halfway through playing over the airwaves sounds familiar, something acoustic with a low, folksy beat and a deep voice singing about places that feel like home. It's a bit amusing to me this is the song the radio host chose to play the morning after half of our ranch was burned to nothing, a little coincidence by fate or destiny or God or whoever controls the things on earth.

Home, like a sunset or the daybreak when I met you or

Home, make me safe and keep me warm for all the nights I can't forget

And don't release me, hold me closer, make me feel like I can't regret

Because home is where I need you.

The keys dangle from the ignition. The words to the song break me down from the inside out, reminding me how alone I actually am. In front of me, the still-illuminated hospital symbol hangs above the emergency room doors, beckoning to me and my dark past. The last time I entered an emergency room, I never actually intended on seeing the inside of the building, never mind leaving it.

But here I am.

As I sit and think, the music flipping over to a ghostly chorus, my chest tightens, and goose bumps cover my skin. A shiver runs up my spine and cascades over my arms, out of my control and despite the raging heat of the Alabama summer. The voice of the singer, deep and heavy, sinks down into my bones with the weight of an ocean tide.

I pull the keys from the truck, climb out, and slam the door. The morning sun crests over the roof's edge as I jog across the gravel parking lot with my phone in hand, the screen black. The long glass doors of the emergency room slide open as I approach, a blast of cool air hitting me in the face, and I rush to the information desk without so much as grabbing a number to tell me where I fall in line.

"Hi, my dad—Thomas Westhaver—was just brought in after a fire." I spit the words out slowly and then all at once. "And his ranch hand, Levy Rider. He's here too."

The gray-haired woman behind the desk barely looks up, tapping away on her computer. There's a pause, punctuated by little clicks of the keyboard. As I look around, there actually isn't a machine to take line numbers from. The emergency room is entirely empty. It feels wrong; the ER in Michigan was frequently packed twice over.

"Mr. Westhaver is still being evaluated, but we have a room prepped for him on floor five if you want to go up to the waiting area. Mr. Rider is in triage."

"Thanks." I nod to the woman. A name tag reading

Rita is askew across the left side of her chest, and she doesn't bother to respond as I walk across the atrium to the elevators. There's a lift already waiting on the ground floor, and I punch the big black 5 button with my thumb as the doors close me in. The whole ride up I think about texting Levy and yelling at him for being so reckless, big capital letters over the face of my screen, but I don't work up enough courage by the time the big double doors open and I'm faced with another receptionist.

"You're here for Mr. Westhaver?" A younger woman speaks from behind a glass partition. "Rita let me know you were on your way up. Waiting room is down at the end of the hallway. Follow the blue squares."

"Thanks."

Down by my feet, a series of colored shapes lead to various parts of the floor, just like at the hospital in Michigan. I try not to think about it as I march down the corridor to another empty room. Part of me wonders if this is a bad sign, the emptiness all over, like something I'd see in a movie right before the whole place would be taken over by zombies or vampires or zombie-vampires. My mother always did say my imagination was a little bit overactive, but since Fitz and everything else went down, I don't think I've had much of an imagination at all.

I sit, restless, in the quiet waiting room for fifty-two minutes, or three complete magazine readings, according to the clock on the wall of the blue-and-gray painted room. At minute fifty-two a man in a long white coat comes to see me, extending one of his hands. In the other is a tablet.

"You must be Mr. Westhaver's daughter. Mr. Rider told us you'd be arriving. I'm Dr. Brown. We have your father in room 515 down the hallway if you'd like to go in and see him. I will warn you he's not awake—he's sustained some serious injuries when the beam fell on him. We've called his next of kin for power of attorney."

The look I give Dr. Brown must be a blank one because he doesn't bother to continue his explanation. Instead, he offers me a gentle smile.

"I'll take you to see him if you'd like. We're working on getting your dad's paperwork filled out, and you can be assured we're giving him the best care."

I nod again. I'm at a loss for words, just like I was on the airplane when that Chatty Cathy wouldn't stop showing me pictures of the cheese-garbled baby Max.

Dr. Brown's white coat shifts with his movements as I follow him down the corridor. Sunshine flows in through the span of eight-foot windows at the back of the building while the wall overlooks a lush backyard garden, the emerald green of the grass thick and luscious unlike the cropped fields of the ranch, telling me someone comes and cares for the flowers and grounds on a regular basis. They're more for show than for work, unlike the paddocks of the stable, and the picnic tables dotting the paths are already populated.

Dr. Brown slides the door open. "A button by the bed will call a nurse if you find you need anything. Don't hesitate to press it, all right?"

"Okay."

He gives me another rehearsed smile before turning away, ducking into room 513 with a greeting. I suddenly smell that astringent hospital scent, and it sticks to my nose and my memories like a wildfire burning in my soul. The memory hurts, like so many of my memories do.

Past the curtain at the side of the room is my father, bandaged and hooked up to machines I don't understand. It's odd, being on this side of the medical situation, seeing someone I know stuck to devices that beep and light up and measure. All I can do is sit at his side and pray to anything and hope somebody out there hears me and grants my wish. I promise unattainable things—I'll never complain again, so long as he's okay. I'll always wear my seatbelt, so long as he's okay. I'll start community service, I swear.

So long as he's okay.

That's what my mother did. I heard it, and I'm not sure she knew it. She promised she'd be a better person—a better parent—if I survived that first night. That was the night she first suggested a change of scenery, a summer stay on a run-down ranch in God-knows-where Alabama.

When I came around, my father offered over the phone.

When he offered, I blamed him. I told him if he had been around more, this never would have happened. I said if he hadn't moved to another state, then maybe my life wouldn't be so messed up. I always knew nothing that happened was his fault, not even for a second. I was projecting my anger and embarrassment and guilt onto him, convincing myself what happened was anybody's fault but Fitz's because I was still compelled to believe he could do no wrong.

It was like a sickness, and maybe in some ways it still is.

I cross the room slowly, taking in the scene in front of me. A flowered chair is in the corner of the room, and I make myself comfortable in it, staring at my resting father in front of me, everything but his face tucked away under stark sheets and a blue, striped blanket. He looks small there on the bed, which is some kind of an illusion. I'm just starting to watch the intravenous line drip down to the tubing when a new shadow appears in the doorway.

Levy.

Chapter 13

The tears that stream down my face at the moment I see Levy aren't the same kind as the ones that trickled over my cheeks when I watched Tin Star burn to the ground. They aren't even similar to the ones that graced me when I found out I'd be sent to Alabama for the summer. And they certainly aren't identical to the ones that welled in my eyes when I tried to end my own life because of Fitz. Instead, these tears are relieved—relieved that this boy before me made it through the fire, saving my father, and is healthy and well enough to stand, sooty and raven-haired in the stark white of the hospital room.

I try to say his name, but the word doesn't come out, instead holing up in my throat as I rush across the room to wrap my arms around his waist.

"It's okay, Mo," he mumbles into my hair. "Everything is fine now."

I want to believe him, I really do, but I'm crying too much to think of anything else. I didn't want to cry in front of him earlier, but I'm crying in front of him now because there's nothing else I can do about it. And he doesn't seem to care—not in the way I thought he would care, not like how Fitz cared whenever I'd have tears running down my face when he'd hit me just one extra time to teach me a lesson. Those tears meant something different to Fitz. These ones appear to mean something more to Levy.

"Are you okay?" I choke the words out and try to catch my breath as he rubs one wide hand over my back. "Dad's, well—"

"I'm fine. I swear it. Don't you be worrying your pretty head about me." The corners of his mouth quirk upward as if he wants to smile, but it's not the right time. "Your father's a strong man, Morrigan. He'll pull through this just like he pulls through everything else."

Everything else. Meaning me.

Levy takes my hand and leads me back toward the flowered chair in the corner of the room.

"Aren't you supposed to be in a bed yourself?" I ask, taking a seat. "I mean, smoke inhalation isn't something you want to mess with."

"I'm fine. Really. The paramedics cleared me halfway here. I'm more worried about you."

I shrug, scratching at the back of my neck with one hand. The skin still feels hot but also raw, like the fire's burned off the top layer. "I'm worried. That ranch was Dad's dream, you know? I mean, I guess I didn't really understand it until I came around to see it, but I don't know what he's going to do now."

"We'll rebuild it," Levy replies without any hesitation. "Tin Star Ranch isn't a place. It's a feeling. It's a family."

A family. I feel like I haven't had one of those in a long time. Sure, Mom is my mom and all, and we had a house back in Michigan, but it wasn't home anymore. It hadn't been home for a long time. It was more like a prison.

Levy pulls a second flowered chair over from the other side of the room to sit next to me. We're quiet for a long time, long enough that the sun is high over the trees out the big window. Long enough that I think I fall asleep for a while, my hand slipped in between Levy's fingers like it's belonged there since the beginning of time. I only come around from my daze once he squeezes my thumb, so gently I almost don't even notice it. When I look up at him, he gives a nod toward the bed where my father's eyes are finally open.

"I'll give you two some time," he murmurs, unraveling himself from my arm.

Dad smiles at the two of us, watching Levy cross the room before he speaks. "Hi, Mo." His voice croaks, like he's still all stuffed up with smoke under the head bandage.

I picture his lungs all crinkled up like two big cigarettes, and more tears flood my eyes.

"Don't cry, please. Please don't cry."

For a moment, the moment it takes me to cross the hospital room and sit on the edge of the bed, I'm mad. I'm so mad at my father for running into the barn to save those stupid horses. Then I remember the instant the mares and their babies came out of the burning stable, following Dad blindly out past the flames. They're not dumb animals—they're trusting ones. They know who can save them. And maybe, like a horse, I know who can save me.

"I thought I was going to lose you," I say, toying with the edge of the striped blanket. "I just got you back, and I thought I was going to lose you again."

My father reaches out a scalded red hand to brush a tear off my cheek. "Oh, sweetheart. I never went anywhere. And I never will."

There's a sniffle then, and when I look up, Dad's

crying too.

The last time I remember my father crying was at Auntie Irma's funeral after she got hit by a car in that crosswalk when I was six. She was somewhere downtown, on her way home from work, when a bus turned a corner and totally swiped her off the edge of the sidewalk. She was Dad's only sister, and I think they had been close growing up. I didn't have siblings, so I didn't understand the loss at that point, other than I wasn't going to get comic books at Christmastime anymore. But I think I understand loss now, and with loss, I understand hope and forgiveness.

"I'm sorry." Another trickle of water rolls down my face. "I'm so sorry for everything."

"I'm sorry too, Mo. I should have been there for you instead of trying to catch some pipe dream." Daddy chokes and coughs for a second before he finishes. "I should have seen how much you were hurting and how much that boy was hurting you. I was so wrapped up in my own world that I don't think I really understood the consequences of letting you and your mother go."

"It wasn't a pipe dream, Dad. It was a real one. One you turned into something really special." I smile between the tears.

"Thanks," he murmurs, stifling another cough. "I was hoping it would be something like that for you too."

There's a light tap at the door before it opens, Levy and Dr. Brown standing under the threshold.

"Ah, Thomas. You're awake. Mind if I run a couple of quick checks?" The doctor seems unaffected by the come-to-Jesus moment my father and I just had.

"Sure," Dad replies, adjusting his position on the

bed so he's sitting up a little more as the doctor approaches. He definitely winces as a bandaged hand comes out from underneath the sheet to help him move.

"Do you need help?" I ask, rising from my seated position and reaching for my father's fluffed pillows. One final tear cascades down my jaw and drips on the hem of my shirt.

"I'm okay, Mo. Really."

"Well, Thomas—we'll talk about that," Dr. Brown states as he tucks the clipboard under his arm. "As a precaution, we'd like to keep you here for a few days for observation and treatment. Some of those burns are pretty nasty, and we want to be sure they're on the mend before we send you back home. You're lucky you weren't hurt worse than you are. Running into a burning building is no joke."

"Can't leave the animals in there," my father notes, grimly. "I'd rather two burnt hands than twenty dead horses."

There's so much finality in his statement that we don't say anything for a moment as Dr. Brown hums over the moving screens, measuring Dad's body in all kinds of different ways I don't understand.

Levy doesn't leave the doorway. "Mo?" He gestures to me. "Maybe we should—?"

Dad glances over at Levy and then back at me again as Dr. Brown starts to check the IV line. "You both should go back," he suggests. "Start to take care of things as best you can. See how much of a mess we're in. Check over all the horses, call the vet, that sort of thing."

"Are you sure?" Levy straightens up from the doorway. "I can take care of all that if Mo wants to stay."

"I'm sure." Dad looks toward me. "Morrigan, you go with Levy. Make sure everything's okay. And call your mother."

Dr. Brown clears his throat. "We called Mrs. Westhaver initially for a POA, Thomas. She indicated she'd be on the next flight out. We weren't sure when you were going to come around."

My father lets out a little smile I don't think I'm supposed to notice. "Call your mother, Morrigan. She's going to come anyway, but tell her I'm fine. Everyone's fine."

"Okay," I mumble, not wanting to leave my father in this empty, white room. I want to hug him and tell him I'm sorry and never let go. But that will have to wait for all the burns to heal, inside and outside.

Levy places his hand between my shoulder blades. "We'll come back for supper. You rest, and we'll get you a status update."

Dad nods, and Dr. Brown gives us a courteous smile before turning back to a page in the clipboard he's retrieved. My eyes feel itchy as I leave the room like I'm going to cry again, but nothing's left to come out of my tear ducts. I'm all empty, devoid of liquid, kind of like I'm a sponge that's been all wrung out.

And I'm tired.

I hand the truck keys over to Levy, who lets out another pained cough he tries to hide from the desk receptionist.

"Can you drive?" I ask, my voice quiet.

"I can."

The drive back to what's left of Tin Star is quiet, but not a pained sort of quiet where things are awkward

125

between the people holding it. Rather, the silence is welcome, as if the ringing of the sirens and screaming of horses from early in the morning still echoes in our ears and gives us both headaches. The red flashing lights, gray smoke, and dark skies have faded into a sunny afternoon, the plumes of smoke that usually hung on the distance now appearing to have retreated with the rain from the day before.

But one other thing sneaks in amongst the thoughts of the fire, and that's what happened between Levy and me in my bedroom just before everything fell apart.

My state of contemplation must be so thick Levy can touch it, because we're nearly all the way back to the ranch when he speaks. "What're you thinking about?"

What am I not thinking about?

"Nothing. Everything. Last night. This morning." I gesture generally around the truck with my hand. I notice for the first time an exploded burn on the side of one of my fingers where I grabbed the hot metal of a horse halter. It stings, a little, but mostly it feels numb. Like the rest of me.

"You know, I think we ought to talk about last night. Maybe not now, but eventually."

"Eventually," I agree as we turn into the driveway. The gravel crunches a familiar song underneath the truck tires, reminding me of the very first day I got to the ranch. Only now, the view is different. In the distance where the stable used to stand is a half-collapsed mountain of wet, burnt timber. The horses are about as far away in the field as they can get, nibbling tentatively at the grass on the edges of the fence line.

We pull up next to the house, and I sigh.

"Guess we'll start with the back paddock with the babies and move from there? There's a first aid kit in the office in the house."

"Okay."

"Okay." Levy heaves open the door, pushing a strand of black hair behind his ear before he gives me a little smile. "Hey, Mo?"

"Hmm?" I slam the truck door, and the sound gets absorbed into the sunshine.

"I don't regret it."

A little smile creeps across my face at the memory of what happened in the dark of my bedroom. The way it felt when Levy's lips brushed my neck, the sensation I got up my spine when his hands slipped over my stomach. I don't regret it either. I thought I might, even though I wouldn't have told him that. A piece of me considered if maybe I could replace Fitz's touches with Levy's, but it only took seconds for me to realize that though Fitz's pain has dulled, Levy's truth outweighs it all. And maybe I've learned a little bit about trust from Stormy.

"Neither do I," I reply.

We don't talk much about us after that moment, the horses taking priority over everything else. I collect the first aid kit from inside the house, the case of medical supplies not seeming quite big enough for all the animals we're going to have to take care of. As I get out in the field, though, Levy's on his cell phone with the vet, making appointments for whoever is on the other end of the line to come out and check all the horses over just in case. My heart does a little jump in my chest when I hear Levy's deep and authoritative voice on the cell. Everything is in good care when placed in his large hands.

Myself included.

Ducking under the fence, I whistle to Stormy who immediately looks up and gives a familiar nicker. The mare ambles over to where I'm walking, snorting at the air and then snuffling at me for the baby carrots I stuffed in my pocket when I was in the house.

"Hey, girl," I murmur, stroking the horse's mane with one hand as I hold a carrot out flat for her to eat. "Are you okay?"

Stormy crunches a response as I run my fingers over her coat, looking for sore spots just like Levy and Dad had taught me to do with Rebel when he took a bad tumble in the west field. I slip my hands down her legs to feel for any cuts or scrapes from her escape from the fire, while she stands quietly at the edge of the field with a sigh.

When Levy hangs up the phone, he gives me a little wink and nods toward the mares with their babies. We walk across the pasture with the sun hanging hot overhead, my hair already sticking to my forehead. But Levy doesn't seem to care. He slips a hand into mine as we walk off into the distance like we're ending some western romance film.

By the time we've done what we need to do with the horses, bandaging a couple of legs and putting ointment on a few cuts and scrapes, the moon is looming up in the sky, and the temperature has dropped at least ten degrees. Little early stars dot the twilight while cotton-candy clouds hang on the forests to the far north.

Levy looks up at me from Indy's side, spotting white cream on the horse's hock, and brushes his hair from his eyes. "I think we're done." He lets out a deep breath.

"Not too bad, considering."

He grins, brushing some dust off his arm. "The barn's a write-off, but the important things are safe. The living, breathing things. We can replace stalls and hay and a roof."

"What if it storms again?" I furrow my brow. "What will the horses do without a barn?"

"They're outdoor animals, Mo. They'll find shelter in the trees. They'd rather be in the rain than in the stalls, for the most part. I don't think after what we got last night there might be anything soon anyway. Plus, Declan, Ranger, and I have been meaning to build some three-sided shelters in the larger paddocks. We might just have to do that first."

"I can help," I offer, and he lets out a little chuckle.

"You know, only a little while ago you barely wanted to be here."

"Honestly, I don't think I wanted to be anywhere. I didn't think anything could fix me."

"You're not broken, Morrigan. You're strong and wild and free, just like that horse of yours. I think she's taught you more about yourself than you're willing to let on."

I think about the last number of weeks with Stormy, following along on the trails to Colbourn Creek, learning to duck under branches, and remembering to carry a hoof pick with me in my saddlebag. I've learned to be slow and careful and quiet, to talk without yelling, to feel without being guilty of having emotions, and to trust without asking for anything more than trust in return.

Levy's right. Stormy did this. The ranch did this. I'm not healed, but I'm getting better.

Chapter 14

The house is understandably quiet when we head back in, soot and sawdust and pieces of burnt hay from my boots on the entryway mat. Without thinking much more of it, I pull out the vacuum cleaner from the hallway closet and suck up all the debris and remnants of the fire in the house while Levy bangs around in the kitchen with only the small range light for the oven on.

"How hungry are you?" he asks, his voice muffled by the walls and the clanging of the vacuum as I shove it back into the closet. The house still smells like smoke, not birthday cake kind of smoke but rather like broken dreams and sweat and tears.

My stomach growls an appropriately timed response. "I could eat."

"There's lasagna in the freezer. Why don't I cook it up and chill a bottle of wine while you get cleaned up?"

I look down at myself, covered in dirt and dust and smelling like some unappealing combination of horse and lemon deodorant. "I'd like that."

The idea of dinner alone with Levy and some wine sounds like just the thing I need after all this. Just a moment to be ourselves and forget that Dad's in the hospital, and my mother is probably on her way to Alabama right now. I can't picture her here with these cowboys, but then again, I couldn't picture myself here either. I'm not sure she's ever seen a horse in real life, let alone ridden one. Though my father grew up on a farm in Georgia, so perhaps anything truly is possible.

I lock myself in the bathroom and turn the shower water up to scalding before ripping off my dirty clothes and jumping under the stream.

Hot water cascades over my shoulders, drumming a tympanic beat on my skin as it washes away the dust and grime of the hospital, the fire, and the day. I twist the handle up as far as I can stand the temperature, my skin red and prickling with heat, while puffs of steam rise above me to coat the glass door. Closing my eyes and holding my breath, I stand with my face under the showerhead, trying to drown away my worries about the ranch, my father, and everything else in between. I must stay like that for a full thirty seconds, maybe more, hair sticking down on my forehead and waiting for a scrub with some of Dad's weird-smelling charcoal shampoo. Then I allow myself to breathe, once the choking feeling of not having enough air has dissipated into a knot in my throat.

I could have lost everything today. I could have been on the next flight back to Michigan, without a father, without Levy, without Stormy or Tin Star Ranch. It all hits me in one second, water pelting me like watery punctuation, and exhaustion and overwhelmed-ness accenting my emotions. The knot in my throat turns into a boulder, and then the boulder weighs me down, sinking my quaking body to the floor of the shower in a puddle of tears. I sob, heaving heavy, trying my hardest to hide the sound of crying by stuffing my fist in my mouth and biting down on my knuckles until I can't stand it any longer.

The water runs until I've used up all the heat, and

then I leave the frigid shower raining down on my shivering body. Time passes slowly, then quickly, then slowly again, the timed bathroom fan eventually turning off and telling me I've been in here for at least half an hour. I don't care. I'll live in here forever if it means I never have to experience the pain I felt today ever again.

A knock at the door scares me, but I don't respond.

Then a second knock, with Levy's voice. "Mo?"

I don't want him to see me crying, so I try to croak out some words, but my mouth doesn't want to work. Nothing about me wants to work anymore. I'm nearly a puddle going down the drain, a melted shell of a human being with nothing left.

A little creak of a door just then, and a brawny shadow slips through the opening before closing it over.

"Levy?" I try to wipe away some of the steam on the frosted door, but I can't see anything much outside from a silhouette. Ice-cold water hammers my scalp, giving me a headache, but nothing is enough pain to heal me or make me whole again. And as I think of this, I'm desperately depressed, and the rhythm of sobs starts hitting me again, louder this time and with nothing to mute them.

"Jesus Christ, Morrigan." Levy rips open the shower door, nearly tearing it off the hinges. He jumps in underneath the spray without even a moment of hesitation at my naked body, twisting the knob to the off position, soaking his clothes immediately down to the bone. Reaching over me in one fluid motion, he grabs an oversized towel from the rack next to the bathtub. He wraps me up in the blue fuzziness, and my shivers echo through both of our bodies as he sits on the wet floor and pulls me close.

"It's going to be okay," he murmurs, his voice low and soothing. "I'm okay. Your dad's okay."

We don't speak after this, not for a while. We just sit on the tiled floor, bodies curved around puddles and each other, and simply exist in the quiet of my occasional hiccup. He strokes my wet hair while I take deep breaths, and it strikes me I don't feel stupid for crying—not in front of Levy. We're whole when we're together, two circles joined together to make an infinity sign. Because maybe that's what love is—two entire beings making the best of everything, together.

I start to shiver again by the time I'm ready to get out, my words shaking as well. "Please don't leave me alone here tonight."

He offers me a gentle smile. "I won't."

The floor is sopping wet when I get out, the water having escaped from the open door before he was able to turn the knob to shut it off. My feet leave prints on the tiled floor all the way to the bath mat, where I stand and allow myself to drip for a few moments before he pulls his drenched shirt over his head. He's just starting to undo the button of his jeans when he catches my glance. My teeth are chattering from the cold shower, and my heart is hammering some kind of rock song in my ribcage. My reaction must make him take a pause for his actions, because that's exactly what he does.

"Maybe you should find something warm to put on," he suggests, his voice gentle and soft as he wrings the water from the ends of his hair onto the shower floor. "The lasagna is almost done, and I think the last thing we need is the smell of something else burning."

"Okay."

I feel like an empty, gray blob as I walk out into the hallway, my body tired from crying and existing and the entire last twenty-four hours. But as soon as I get to the doorway of my bedroom, I hear someone coming through the front door with a familiar creak of the hinges.

"Hello? Morrigan?"

"Mom?" I peek my head around the corner of the hall.

"Oh, hi, honey." Mom kicks off a pair of white sneakers, now covered in driveway dust, and places her flowered suitcase against the wall. "How are you making out?"

Keys for a rental car jingle as she sets them on the key rack by the front door like she lives here.

"I'm fine—I meant to call you to tell you everything's fine." I tighten the towel around my chest and swipe a droplet of water.

Mom's brow crinkles. "You don't sound fine, Mo. Were you crying? Your face is all puffy and red."

"I just got out of the shower—"

The oven timer dings, interrupting my sentence, and a half a second later, a shirtless Levy with a towel around his waist opens the bathroom door. "That's the lasagna, Mo—"

"Well, hello." My mother raises an eyebrow, looking at a soaking wet Levy and then back at me in my blue towel. "I hope I'm not interrupting."

"Mom!" I squeal, shoving at Levy to try and make him disappear from this awkward moment altogether. "It's not what you think. We just got in from the horses and—"

Levy laughs, a deep and throaty laugh that

135

resonates through the quiet of the house. "Nice to see you again, Mrs. Westhaver."

"Please, Levy. Call me Molly like we talked about last time." Mom climbs the single step to the main level of the house and heads toward the kitchen, past the two of us. "How's your community service working out? You must be almost done."

I'm pretty sure my jaw drops all the way to the floor.

"It's been over for about four and a half months now," Levy mumbles as if he's trying to hide the words from me and only have them reach my mother's ears. The term *community service* is ringing so loud in my head I'm not sure they get through anyway. "I decided to stay was best."

The memory of asking him how long he's worked at the ranch back when I first arrived is suddenly fresh again, especially the way he responded; hesitant.

"Community service?" I croak, pulling at the damp towel around my torso.

"Yes," Mom calls as she pulls the lasagna out of the oven, the smell of bubbling cheese cascading over the room and out to the hallway. "Sometimes those things happen. Now, how's about the two of you get dried off and come eat?"

Tears prickle at the corners of my eyes as I take off down the hallway.

Community service. Levy was brought here to do community service. Like, he committed some kind of crime and was sent to Tin Star in order to be rehabilitated, like a horse, only worse.

"Mo—" he starts, but I slam the door in his face. I can't look at him right now. I just can't. He lied to me by omission, as Dad would have called it in his legal language. He made a point of choosing not to tell me he's at the ranch because he was forced into it, and I made a point of telling him my innermost secrets.

We're on opposite sides of the same door again, exactly as we were when I told him about Jessie.

"Morrigan, please open the door."

I don't say anything, but I stand there in the middle of the room like an absolute idiot as if I'm waiting for him to burst in and try and explain everything. But he won't; he's not Fitz. He wouldn't even open that door without my permission, even though the thing isn't locked. It's just not in his nature.

"Mo, I was going to tell you. I swear it. It just—it was never a good time."

"Never a good time? Do you think me telling you about what happened to me fell at a good time?" The words practically come out with venom attached as I throw down the towel and pull on a pair of jean shorts and a yellow T-shirt.

"I know, I mean—I guess I thought maybe if I never mentioned it, it would just go away. I didn't want you to think I was a criminal like Fitz."

Fitz's name stabs me right in the heart, and a steady stream of tears starts to fall over my cheeks, my face hot and my chest tightening. "What do you think I'm thinking now, Levy? That you're just some good guy in the wrong place at the wrong time? Like hell." I throw a shoe at the door, and it bangs off the wood before bouncing to the floor.

"Maybe I should just go," his muffled voice says from the hallway. "You've got your mom here. I think you'll be all right."

I don't want him to go, but I don't want him to stay either. I want him to tell me what's going on, and I want my father to be all right, and I want Tin Star to go back to yesterday when everything was fine. But maybe destruction is what we need to grow, like those trees Mrs. Ferguson told us about in third grade that have seeds that become exposed by wildfires.

Maybe my life has been a wildfire, burning until this moment and knocked out with the moment Tin Star turned to ash.

So I open the door.

"I'm not fine," I murmur, just loud enough for Levy to be able to hear me. "Please don't go."

He pulls me into his chest, the beige towel he was wrapped in before replaced by a dry pair of jeans and a black shirt he found God-knows-where in the house. The scent of shower water clings to his skin, combined with the smell of the lasagna from down in the kitchen. Underneath it all is the aroma of sunshine, hay, and that little bit of bourbon I can never place. It has to be some kind of cologne, a body wash, something. Something that sticks just as well as the horses do.

"It was at a bar," he starts, running his fingers down the back of my neck as he keeps me close. "All horrible things start at bars, and this was just another incident that probably could have been avoided without fake IDs and a whole lot of alcohol."

"What happened?"

"My brother got into a fight with some of the guys from Alamo City. Knocked a guy out with one punch and got swarmed by the other drunks who were with him. Long story short, I saw red and ended up ripping everyone apart. That's the only part the cops saw, and I got arrested."

"But why'd your brother punch someone in the first place?" I lean back in his arms and stare at his gentle eyes, unable to picture him in a fight with anyone.

"With Kiel, it's hard to know. There's never a good reason. We didn't talk much before that. We definitely don't talk much now."

I sigh and lean back against him.

"I'm sorry. I just—with Fitz and everything I just...I know I should trust you. I do trust you. I think the whole thing just caught me off-guard. I'm sorry. I'm so sorry."

"Don't be sorry, Mo. I should have said something earlier. Or ever."

A little smile crawls across my face, the dried tears on my cheeks feeling like they're going to crack the skin.

Mom pokes her head around the hallway wall, interrupting our moment. "Lasagna's ready, you two. Just the right temperature to eat. I've set the table."

Levy pecks the top of my head with his lips before letting me loose. "You hungry? It's been a long day."

I nod, scratching at the side of my face where the salt from the tears is itching me. When my gaze sweeps past him, it lands on my mother in the distance, who is looking at the two of us with a sort of quiet contemplation as we head down the hallway.

"So who wants to be the first to tell me what exactly is going on here?"

"Nothing," I say quickly, looking over at Levy who gives me the sweetest, broadest smile.

"Everything," he replies.

Mom laughs the familiar, tinkling laugh I used to hear her use on the phone when she'd talk to my father. Now I hear those calls from the other end, Dad chuckling as something amusing is said on the opposite end of the line. I've been listening to them for years now, ever since they separated, and it always makes me wonder why they don't love each other anymore.

"Well, I mean, I guess something. Nothing is kind of an understatement. But I'm fine, Mom. Really. Everything is fine now."

My mother hands me over a plate of warm lasagna, but she's not looking at me. She's looking at Levy. "Is everything fine?" she asks him like she doesn't trust me, cutting another slice of the casserole and piling some salad next to the slab of cheese and noodles.

He takes a deep breath. "Mo's really grown here, Molly. I'm sure Tom told you she's been working with her own horse. And she's talking in full sentences, which is an improvement from the first day I saw her. It was like pulling teeth to get her to say anything."

Mom smiles at Levy like they've known each other more than just this moment.

My brow furrows before I even realize it. "How do you two know each other, anyway?" I set my plate down on the wooden farmhouse table.

"It's not like I haven't been here before, Mo." Mom takes her own seat at the head of the table where my father usually sits. It's strange not to see him there, cutting up a steak or shoveling some oddly cut potatoes into his mouth. He's definitely not the best cook in the world, but then again neither was Mom, and we made out okay.

But the thought of Dad lying in the hospital bed,

unconscious, floods tears into my eyes again. My face turns red. I know it does because heat rises up the back of my neck and settles like fire in my cheeks.

"Oh, Morrigan Rose—it's like Levy said," my mother croons. "Everything's going to be okay. We're all together now, and we'll take care of the horses until your father's all better. He just needs time."

Levy reaches for my hand across the table, not even bothering to hide our connection from my mother. "Remember Stormy when she first came here, Mo? She needed time to heal too. Just like you. And now, just like your dad. Remember what I said before about Tin Star?"

I nod, sniffling. "It's a family, not a place."

"Exactly. And right now, this family—me, you, Declan, Stormy, the trail riders—we all need to stick together to make sure everyone makes it through this change. Because that's what this is, change. Everything goes through it, and now Tin Star is as well. And we will grow and move on and eventually this won't be anything but dust on our boots, you know?"

A little sigh escapes my throat as I use my other hand to toy with the edge of the plate. For a second time, my stomach growls, and I can't help but wonder if maybe some of Dad's home-cooked lasagna might solve something. It might not solve everything, but at least at this moment, I can feel like I'm the one in control of this part of my world.

Chapter 15

When my alarm goes off at five in the morning, the lights in the kitchen are already on, and the smell of bacon sizzling has crept the gap under my door. Declan's heavy voice makes its own way down the hall, mixed with Levy's familiar tone. Every once in a while, I can hear the sound of my mother's laugh. It's such an unfamiliar way to wake up here on the ranch that I lie in bed and absorb the moment for a little bit, before Levy's footsteps creep down the hall, and he knocks on the door frame.

"Mo? Are you coming?"

The little birds chirping outside my open window sound like they're going to answer for me, flitting around in the bush outside of the bedroom. I know I shouldn't have the window open when the air conditioning is on, but something about the sound of nature this early in the morning helps with the anxiety I used to feel. Reaching over to the bedside table, I switch on the little lamp I sometimes read by. When I look over at my phone, a string of old messages from Fitz is bright on the screen. I looked at them last night again, but just for a second.

One second. Or ten.

"Yeah, just a minute."

There's a subtle pause, like it's been placed in the conversation for emphasis. "Can I come in?"

I have nothing to hide from Levy, except maybe those messages. He's seen me at both my worst and my best, and even though my hair is probably sticking up every single way imaginable, I know he doesn't care. And the fact that I already don't care says something comforting to me as well.

But I still flip the phone screen over. "Mhmm."

The bedroom door opens slowly, Levy peeking in. He has his hair in a bun at the back of his head, pulled tight all the way around and showing off his chiseled jaw and just a hint of stubble. "Good morning, sunshine. I love the rock star look you've got going on with your hair. It's very—"

"Don't even say it." I yawn, the words coming out of my mouth all stretched out. "It's like you always say. The horses don't care what you look like."

"Fair enough. Vet's coming out to have a look over the horses this morning. Your mom's making breakfast, and then Declan and I are going to get started on hauling water and redoing bandages and all that. I think she wants you to go to the hospital with her, so you're free from barn duty until later."

"Where's Ranger?" I crumple myself under the blankets a little more as he smirks. I feel like I'm in a warm cocoon, and I don't exactly want to leave just yet.

"Going to Alamo City later to get some insurance papers. I guess he knows the guy who runs the place, so he's going to try and get all that organized. We've got this, Mo."

"I know." I smile, wriggling my way out from underneath the sheets to expose a pair of pink cotton shorts and my tank top from two years ago. "I'm just checking up on your work, remember?"

He rolls his eyes, the action more playful than sarcastic. "Of course, I remember. You, on your first day here, coming to make sure I wasn't messing anything up."

"Well, I'm checking in again, cowboy. Making sure everything's just so."

He watches me for a second. I watch him right back, observing the way he stands in the door just like he stood in front of me with Rosie that day I reluctantly rolled into Tin Star Ranch. He's wearing that same T-shirt and jeans combination he had on that afternoon, and if I didn't know any better, I'd swear he lived in the cowboy hat in his hand. I know better now. I just didn't then.

He sets the hat down on the shelf by the wall, takes a step into the room, and shuts the door. He's silhouetted by darkness and the little yellow light of the side table lamp, the shadows cascading over his face and arms showing me exactly how broad his shoulders are. I haven't seen this look on his face before, at least not for as long as he's showing it to me now.

"What's going on?" I ask, sitting against the headboard and watching him cross the room.

He takes a seat on the edge of the bed, his weight shifting me to one side of the mattress, and he gives me this shy smile. "I just wanted to tell you again how sorry I am I didn't tell you about the whole community service thing. That wasn't right of me. I think I just thought you had enough going on that you didn't need me as another broken thing on your plate."

"You're not broken, Levy."

"Neither are you, sunshine."

I give him a closemouthed smile because I'm a

little worried about him being so close to me and my morning breath. "Wait, what's with this sunshine business?" I crinkle my face up as I look into his dark eyes.

The corner of his mouth quirks into a smile. "Well, your hair color combined with eight hours against that pillow, the result is a bit like you've got a whole bunch of little sun rays coming from your head."

Bursting into laughter, I pull the feather pillow out from behind my back and whack him with it as hard as I can.

After that, morning after morning, Levy wakes me up with a small knock at the door. I don't know how he does it because my alarm's the thing that's supposed to be waking me, but he finds a way to beat out the alarm and greet me with a coffee or waffles or something my mother's prepared. Of course, she does this because breakfast is the most important meal of the day, and I'd swear that saying came all the way from Michigan just to haunt me.

Clearly though, I didn't give my mom enough credit when I considered what she'd be like on the ranch. She has Declan, Ranger, and Levy off and running each day with some kind of schedule she's got ingrained in her head. Somehow her level of organization around the ranch rivals that of my father, and even though she has no idea what to do when she's handed the lead line of a horse, she does know how to measure out their grain and drive the little tractor around the paddocks to pick up manure.

It's actually a little funny to see her trade her heels and business suits for jeans. She's even managed to dig up some cowboy boots from God knows where. But then again, I guess it was a little funny to see me that way too.

A week or so after the fire, once Mom and I come home for lunch after visiting Dad in the hospital, Levy mentions to me over a bite of a sandwich that Stormy desperately needs a ride. We're sitting on the front porch under the overhang, two cups of coffee on the ledge of the railing, and my socked feet are up on his dusty lap. The sky overhead and out into the fields is gray, but not the ominous gray of the forest fires or the thunderstorms. Just a light gray of high-up clouds that, if it rained, might actually create a rainbow.

"You up for a trail ride? I'd like to see if the creek retained any water," Levy asks, handing over the last bite of ham and cheese sandwich to me.

I promptly stuff it into my mouth, the red pepper jelly Dad likes a little hot on my tongue. "I think so. I mean, do you think Stormy'll be okay?"

He nods. "She'll be fine. She likes to work, and she likes to go do things. I'll bring Rosie, and that'll keep her happy."

"Sure, then." I wipe my hands on my jeans. "It'll be nice to have a different view. Mom's going back to the hospital, but they said Dad should be able to come home tomorrow, so I think I just need a little breather."

"I'm sure they'll understand." He smiles, poking at my socks. "Let's get the horses ready then before it rains."

I stretch over the end of the rocking swing, my sternum cracking as I extend my arms. "Okay."

We gulp down the rest of our cooled-off coffee before we make our way across the drive and toward the back field. The sun's trying to make its way through the overcast sky, little slits of light coming through. Mom's walking back with an empty bucket from one of the paddocks as we pass, and I mention to her about going riding instead of going to see Dad again since he'll be home in the morning. She doesn't seem to mind.

Levy and I are quiet as we fetch Rosie and Stormy, tacking them up in their heavy western saddles amid the ambient noise. The end of the barn with the tack room was conveniently salvaged from the fire, but the boys still went in and pulled all the saddles and brushes and whatnot and placed them in one of the outbuildings for safekeeping. I didn't really like the fact that they all went storming in there to collect their things, but Levy assured me the building was okay to go in on that end just once. I still don't know if I believe him, but it did make me feel better at the time.

Unusually, the trail to Colbourn Creek is damp, the spots of mud sucking against the horses' feet as we walk along the well-worn path toward the generally non-existent water. Levy leads the way because Rosie's the more senior horse, and Stormy's more of a follower than a leader anyway. Because the mares like each other, for most of the ride we're able to amble along side by side, looking off into the trees for damage and deer and other sights we usually point out to the trail riders.

But we're quiet. The world is quiet when I'm with Levy. It's like all the voices inside of my head have gone silent.

"Hey, look." Levy points, Rosie's reins gathered in one hand. I twist my head over to the right and see a little trickle of water through the long grass.

Nicole Bea

"Is that the creek?" I already know the answer to the question before I even asked it. Stormy sneezes a response.

"Want to ride in it?"

"In the water? I mean, can horses even swim?"

"Mo, the water's a foot deep. I don't think it matters, but yes, horses can swim." He gives Rosie a little cluck with his tongue, and she takes off down the trail in a slow jog. "Come on, Mo!"

I gather up my reins just a little bit and squeeze Stormy forward, her smooth gait allowing me to sit tall in the saddle without bouncing too much. Rosie and Levy aren't that far ahead of us, so we catch up quickly, and the horses splash into the slow river without even a second of hesitation. Water droplets fly from their hooves, leaving little wet spots on my boots and up their legs.

"Easy, now." Levy brings Rosie to a halt in the middle of the water, and I let Stormy come to a stop on her own next to the other horse. The sound of trickling and whistling trees is a symphony around the four of us, and the horses' ears twitch lazily as they listen to what it is we're hearing.

"I haven't seen the river this full in a year," Levy notes with a grin, Rosie pawing at the water with her front hoof like she's trying to either dig to the bottom or understand what it is she's standing in. "Trail riders will probably like to come down and ride through the creek. It'll definitely be an attraction to some of our regulars."

"Mrs. Ronsdale will probably have her sister come down to have a look. Too bad she doesn't have the place to have her own horse. She'd be a great owner."

He nods. "I think half of Mrs. Ronsdale coming

148

here is because of your father, Mo. Haven't you noticed she's always thanking him and touching his arm?"

I think back for a second and then laugh. Levy's right. Mrs. Ronsdale from Alamo City probably would marry my dad in an instant if it wasn't so obvious he was still into my mother. And judging from the fact that Mom took time off from her law practice to come down this way, I'd beg to say any different about her feelings as well.

There's a faint ringing just then, and it catches me off guard so much I half jolt out of Stormy's saddle.

"Your phone?" Levy asks as I look around for the source of the noise. I almost don't recognize the tune playing because it's not one of my personalized ringtones.

Stormy reaches her neck down to stick her muzzle in the water, and I loop my reins around the horn before reaching back to unbuckle the flap of the saddlebag. By the time I do so, the ringtone is repeating itself.

I swipe at the screen, the number from Michigan but not one I know offhand. "Hello?"

"Morrigan?" The voice is smooth and familiar and crushes my soul the second I recognize it.

"Fitz?"

Levy practically spins Rosie a full ninety degrees to face me the second I spit out the name. My heart falls down into my toes, which go numb.

"Hi, baby. How are you?"

"Where are you?" I look around, panicking, Stormy sensing my unease by shifting her weight from one side to the other. I don't know why I think Fitz would be here in the woods of Colbourn Creek, but I guess I shouldn't expect anything less from someone like him.

Levy, meanwhile, looks like he's about to jump off his horse and throw my phone into the river, although with the little amount of water washing past us, it probably wouldn't do any good anyway.

"What do you mean, where am I? I'm right where your mother left me. But I got phone privileges, Mo. I can call you now, and nobody has to know." Fitz's voice is that common poison he used to put out, the one where he'd try and tell me I deserved whatever he gave me and tried to make me forgive him.

I'm not going to forgive him this time. I need him away. I need him out of my phone and out of my life. "Don't *baby* me, Fitzgerald. Don't even start. You know there's a restraining order against contacting me. You're where you are for a reason, and I don't need or want you in my life."

Levy grumbles in the background while Rosie inches up so her muzzle is resting on my thigh. "Give me the phone, Morrigan." His words are quiet, but I know what he's doing is for my own protection. He knows I couldn't get rid of all those messages, and I'm sure he knows now that Fitz isn't exactly the easiest person on the planet to delete. But all it takes is that voice, that stupid comfort I feel when I hear it, for my whole world to come crashing down in a mass of tears.

"Who the hell is that, baby? Do you have some other guy with you? You've got to be kidding me. You—"

"I'm calling the cops, Fitz." I try to steady my tremoring voice.

"You're not calling the goddamn cops, you—" Fitz lists out a stream of curse words, the words I'm more familiar with than the smoothness of his voice when I first picked up the phone.

"I'm calling the cops," I repeat, a little stronger this time, and as soon as I get the sentence out, I pull the phone from my ear and punch the end call button. As I wipe tears from my cheeks, the phone slips from my hand and tumbles against the saddle, bouncing underneath Stormy into the water. The screen lights up for a second, and both Levy and I stare at it until the light is replaced by blackness.

As if nothing else could be more perfect, Stormy lifts her foot and stomps it into the water, smashing the device into a billion pieces.

My heart catches in my throat just then, because the messages from Fitz are gone for good. A sense of loss breaks over me, crushing my ribs into what feels like powder. But after the panic recedes, which only takes a second, it strikes me that I don't need those messages anymore. I don't need that phone anymore, because everything I've ever needed is right here on this ranch.

"Morrigan?" Levy uses my real name, which reminds me he's still standing there with Rosie's face next to my knee.

"Yeah?" I look up, absently touching the spot under my eye where Fitz cracked my eye socket such a long time ago now. It takes a second for me to recognize that I've done it, and as soon as I do, I occupy myself with Stormy's reins.

"You did good," Levy notes, poking some numbers into his phone. "But I'm still calling the police."

"Okay."

"You didn't change your number once Fitz got

arrested?"

Now that I think about it, that's something the police and the doctors told me I needed to do, but I never did. At the time I thought I needed those messages, and I think part of me also thought maybe Jessie would call.

She never did.

She probably never will.

Levy gives all the details to the police as we stand there with two quiet horses in the water, the river washing away all the final pieces of Fitz.

Chapter 16

Dad comes back home the next morning after Ranger and I feed the horses and haul the water, the bandage around his skull replaced with a piece of gauze that sticks against his forehead. I can tell the difference in the burns on his hands and arms just in the one day I didn't see him, and he's all smiles as he walks through the front door of the house and plops himself in the kitchen to make a coffee in the coffee machine. My mother follows in behind him, carrying a travel case and a prescription bag from the Alamo City pharmacy down on Timmons Boulevard.

Levy has the day off, but he's offered to take me away from the ranch for the day, which my mother enthusiastically noted would be a great idea. I'm not sure exactly what it is she's thinking because only months ago I was on the verge of ending my own life, but I think perhaps she can see how happy her decision to send me down to Alabama has made me, in the end.

Something else interesting is going on, though. My mother has started unpacking her suitcases. Usually, Mom's the kind of person who lives out of her baggage when she goes away on vacation for a week. But here, she's actually started using the closet in Dad's bedroom, the only extra room not filled with horse paraphernalia and other ranch business. I don't know where she plans on sleeping now that he's home because I can't imagine them sharing a bed.

Or maybe I just don't want to.

Or maybe, more realistically, I do.

Dad gives my mother a kiss on her cheek when she hands him the coffee from the machine, his legs presumably tired from walking and standing after being in bed for so long.

The action makes me smile a little, and I put down the copy of *Black Beauty* I was reading on the couch. "Can I ask you a question?" I blurt out, the inquiry generally meant for the two of them. I twist the band around my wrist a little. I haven't been playing with it nearly as much as I used to. Some days, not this day but other ones, I forget to even put something over my scars at all.

"Sure, Mo. What's up?" Dad rises from his bar stool with a bit of stiffness and ambles over to his favorite chair before plunking down. Mom looks over from her own cup brewing and nods.

"I just—it just seems a little odd that you're still here, Mom. I mean, you've never left your practice for this long."

"Cherie's got things under control there with my clients, Morrigan," Mom replies, the coffee machine whirring in the background as it spits hot water through the pod. "I have all the time in the world to be here and make sure everything's running okay."

"But," I sputter, "this is Dad's ranch, not yours. I mean, I know you've been running some things around here with the guys but—I guess I'm confused."

"About what?" Dad takes a sip of his coffee, steam rising up in front of his face.

"I just, I don't know. I mean, you guys talk all the

time, and you're on the phone laughing with each other, and Mom, you came down here right away when you heard Dad was hurt, but yet you're still not together."

"Oh, Mo." Mom picks up her mug and walks into the living room. "Just because we're not together doesn't mean I don't love your father."

"That works the other way too. I love Molly, very much. But it's not in the way that you belong with someone forever. It's more in the way that we mean something to one another and always will."

"There's different types of love," Mom notes, perching on the arm of Dad's leather recliner. "We don't have the marriage kind of love. We don't even have the kind of connection you have with Levy. We have something different—we have you."

"Wait." Dad crunches up his face as if it's suddenly started to hurt again. "What's this about Mo and Levy?"

"Oh, Tom, don't pretend like you didn't notice something going on between the two of them. It was obvious from the moment I stepped into this house."

She leaves out the part where it was obvious because Levy and I were half-naked coming out of the shower, which I appreciate.

"Okay, well, maybe after I caught them both in Mo's bed the night of the fire—but I potentially tried to block it out of my memory until we could sit down and have a conversation about it. Which is happening, well, right now apparently."

The look my mother gives me could melt glass.

"Oh, Molly, give her a break." My father pats her on the leg. "It's not like you resisted this cowboy when you were eighteen."

She blushes, her rosy complexion turning even more pink than usual.

"*Anyway*," I interrupt, looking down at the cover of *Black Beauty* instead of at my parents. "I guess what you're trying to tell me is you're not getting back together."

My father nearly spits out his coffee while Mom stifles a laugh, turning the sound into a kind of a snort.

"Oh Lord, Morrigan. No, no, we aren't."

The confirmation makes my heart sink a little, even though I knew somewhere deep inside the odds of them becoming a couple again was unlikely.

Before I have a chance to ask any more questions, there's a little knock at the front door before it swings wide open behind the half wall.

"Hey," Levy calls, scuffing his boots on the mat before peering over at the three of us. "Mo, you ready to head out?"

"Yeah," I reply, officially marking my page in *Black Beauty* for me to come back to later.

"Where are you two headed off to, anyway?" Dad asks. The steam fogs up his glasses this time as he holds the cup too long under his nose.

"I thought I'd take Mo to the city for one of Kaiser's famous sandwiches and then head down to the Gulf to the beach and Peace Gardens. Florida's only a couple of hours away. It's more about getting off the ranch than anything else."

"For you or for her?" Mom jokes, rising from the arm of the recliner as the rhetorical question hangs in the air. "Can I get you a coffee to-go?"

"Have one in the truck, but thanks, Molly."

Picking up my little tote bag from the hall, I stuff

my feet into my relatively unworn pair of slip-on shoes I pulled from my suitcase earlier this morning. My cowboy boots have gotten the most wear out of anything this summer, except maybe the pair of dark-wash skinny jeans I love riding in. They're probably permanently covered in horse dirt, but I don't care because I think, in a way, I'm permanently covered in horse dirt too.

"Ready?" Levy grins, one hand on the screen door as the late morning light streams through the front of the house.

"Ready."

The drive to Alamo City has a soundtrack, the crooning voice of some local country artist on the radio as we head toward Kaiser's Sandwiches. I'm not hungry, but Levy's said it's probably good to pick up something for the drive as we have a couple of hours until we make it to the Florida coastline and the Gulf. It feels so strange to be leaving the ranch behind us, the dust from the driveway probably since settled. Once we pick up our two lunches—ham and cheese for me and smoked meat for Levy—we start to make our way down the interstate for the long drive to the beach.

However, maybe twenty minutes go by before Levy takes an exit, pulling off the freeway into what turns into a tiny residential area. "Mind if we make a stop first?" he asks, even though it's probably already too late for me to say no.

"Where are we?"

"This is a little place called Paradise."

I laugh, looking around at the green lawns and little multi-colored houses with gardens all out front. Mailboxes line the narrow road with surnames I've never heard of, until we park on a street called Gardenia in front of a little yellow stucco home with bright white shutters.

Levy switches off his truck and looks at me, expectantly. "I know this is probably a little strange, Mo." His voice is suddenly a bit on the shy side. "But it occurred to me on the way here you've never actually seen where I live. I mean, I'm at your place all the time, but for all you know, I live in some tent on the side of the road until I have to be at the ranch."

A tiny grin cracks across my face as I look out the passenger's side window at the house, all kinds of plants lining the exterior in a variety of colors. The more I look at it, the more it seems like a place Levy would live, little touches everywhere—like a horseshoe on the front door—reminding me of him. "It's so sweet, cowboy. I had no idea you liked to garden. I mean, I presume you're the one taking care of all these plants?"

"I am. Admittedly, it's probably not exactly what you'd think I like to do in my spare time, but there you have it. The gardens were my mother's, and when she and my dad moved to the Keys, they left Kiel and me the house. Kiel took off pretty soon after that, and I didn't see him again until about when I ran into him at that bar before I got arrested."

"Do they ever come back here? Your parents, I mean?"

"Sometimes, in the spring they'll come to see I'm doing okay. But they don't travel much anymore."

I fidget with my seatbelt, unbuckling the snap to turn around all the way. "They know you got arrested, though?" Tilting my head to one side, I try to read his mind before he answers the question.

After a little pause, he unbuckles his seatbelt too before responding. "I think that might be why they don't come back much anymore." He flicks the keys once again in the ignition, and the dull sounds of the radio turn into silence.

Thoughts float around my mind as we sit there with open windows, the breeze billowing softly through the front of the truck before escaping out the opposite side. This moment here feels special. Not that the other moments we shared weren't, but there's a different kind of undertone to this. Levy's being vulnerable with me, personal and surprising, taking me off the ranch only to bring me to the place he calls home away from mine. If the inside reflects anything about him, it will be purposeful and woodsy, simple art and furniture in earthy tones. The kitchen will have pots in the sink and mugs on the counter. The bedroom? Well, that's a space I'm increasingly curious about.

I count the minutes we sit there and stare at the house and each other, two, maybe three moments in time before my voice breaks it. "Levy?"

"Hmm?"

"Can we go inside?"

"In the house?" He sounds amazed at the idea, as if my interest in his home is greater than he expected.

"Sure, I mean, aren't you going to give me a grand tour?" I flash him a bright smile.

"What about Florida and the Peace Gardens?" The grin on his face gives him away. I can tell he would much rather show me around his place than go on a two-hour drive one way, though I'm sure he wouldn't have complained for a second.

"Florida can wait. It's not going anywhere unless

159

global warming hits it in the next hour."

He pauses, hesitant. I can see a myriad of thoughts ticking in his mind, gears moving and shifting around as he tries to think up the right thing to say. It takes him longer than usual.

"What's wrong?"

"It's nothing. It's just that—Mo, we haven't had a lot of time alone. And I have to admit if we go in that house and I show you around and I see you and my bed in the same place, well—" He takes a deep breath, and I know he's going to keep rambling, so I stop him right in his tracks.

"Levy, it's all right."

That sigh he's been holding gets let out. "Is it, though? I mean, just the other day Fitz—"

"Levy, I mean it. What we did the night of the fire wasn't an accident, and I don't regret it. Showing you all my scars made me feel vulnerable enough. Somehow I think you showing me your house is the equivalent."

"I mean," he starts, but I put up my hand to quiet him so I can get my own words out before I lose them.

"You don't have to explain, cowboy. I know all about broken hearts and bruised skin. I know about love and loss and everything in between. And more than anything, more than this summer and every other summer I've ever had, I know one thing's for sure, and it's that I'm ready for whatever comes next."

He reaches over and places his hand on my chin before leaning to my side of the truck and kissing me, softly and passionately. My heart beats a thousand miles a minute, just like it does every time he kisses me, only this time I know it's just the beginning of whatever's going to happen the second we get inside that little, lemony-yellow house.

"There's just one other thing, though, and I wanted to tell it to you first. I was going to wait until after we got back from Florida, but as soon as I saw my exit, I knew I had to tell you now." He leans back across the center console. "Away from the ranch and everything."

"What is it?"

He looks a little sad. "I got another job. In Florida at one of the big equestrian centers. Amberwood in Ocala. It's a little more money, and they will pay for me to take a farrier course, and plus it's close to my parents' place, and Dad's not well, plus Kiel—"

I reply without thinking, even though for a second my whole body is screaming at me about the idea of letting Levy go. "You should take it."

"Really?" His surprise is evident, as if he expected me to fight him on one of his own life decisions.

"Sure, I mean, Florida's not that far away." I shrug.

We pause, and time stops, the seconds turning into little droplets of fast-moving water because suddenly our time together has a limit.

"Only eight hours with traffic." His voice is flat.

I nearly choke but do my best to make it sound like I'm clearing my throat. Little tears dot the corners of my eyes, and I blink them away. I never should have expected he would stay at Tin Star forever. I don't know what I was thinking, and perhaps I wasn't—too focused on Stormy and the fire and Dad getting better and Mom coming down to Alabama that I missed something that should have been obvious the whole time.

"Eight hours. We can do weekends when you're

not working." I try my hardest to sound chipper, but I know I'm not doing a very good job. Plus, I'm only fooling myself because in the horse business someone's always working.

"That would be nice." Clearly, Levy's trying to fool himself too. "Are you sure about this, Morrigan? I mean, you're going back to Michigan with your mom at some point anyway—"

Am I, though? It's something I neglected to think of throughout the course of the summer because it never really struck me as something impending. But Levy's right, it's coming soon, and my summer in Alabama on Tin Star ranch is coming to a close. I look up at the sun, pinpricks of light hitting my eyes and leaving little white dots like what I used to get when Fitz would hit me on the side of my face. Only this time they aren't met with a physical kind of pain, just an emotional one.

"I guess you're right." I sigh, just for emphasis.

Levy leans back against the headrest. "It's been a great summer, Mo." As if I don't already know that and my heart hasn't already fallen into my shoes.

"Better than I expected."

He offers me a consolation smile, the kind someone gives when they don't know what else to do, before turning the truck engine back on. "Still feel like going to the Gulf?"

I don't, but I say yes anyway because I think I'm in desperate need of some salt air, wild waves, and vitamin sea.

Chapter 17

Levy leaves the next Wednesday. I'm in the front paddock with Stormy and Rosie, reading the end of *Black Beauty*, when he walks by with his reining saddle hanging off his hip. A bridle jingles over his shoulder, and Rosie looks up with a nicker, maybe thinking he's going to take her out on the trail down to Colbourn Creek. However, what Rosie doesn't seem to know is that she's had her last ride with Levy, at least for the summer and maybe forever.

I don't know how to explain it to a horse that their person is leaving, just like I don't know how to explain it to myself that the first person I've trusted in a long time is going away too.

Tucking the corner of the paperback down to mark my place, I shut the book at nearly the last page as Levy approaches. His truck is off to the side of the pasture, and he gives me a little wink as he walks by before opening the passenger's side door to lob the saddle and bridle in. A whole pile of gear is in there, chaps and buckets of brushes and horse boots and cowboy paraphernalia, so much that it can be seen from the window when he shuts the door.

"You're really going," I say, the question coming out as a statement more than anything else.

Levy runs his hand through his long, jet-black hair, messing up the strands so they flip over his forehead.

"I'm really going. But I'll miss it here."

"What will you miss?"

"Oh, Rosie, of course." He smiles, leaning on the fence post between us. "Early mornings at the creek. Your dad's barbecued corn. Riding the fence line at sunset. Shooting the shit with the guys in the barn. Or what's left of the barn."

"Anything else?" I'm prying for an answer I know he's going to give anyway.

"I don't think so." His grin gets wider, and I poke at his side with the corner of Dad's copy of *Black Beauty*.

"Well, in that case," I note, pretending to be haughty, "I don't think I'll miss you either way."

He swiftly pulls the paperback from my hand and drops it in the grass before grabbing me around the waist, the fence between us digging into our chests. My arms slip over the top rail and wrap around his neck, fingers digging into his soft hair and disappearing in the dark tresses. Stormy snorts in the background, her hooves trampling the grass as she makes her way over toward us, the gentle thudding of her feet mimicking the beating of my heart.

"I can't believe you're going to Florida." I sigh, the state name coming out of my mouth all awkward, like I don't really want to say it.

"I can't believe you're going back to Michigan in a couple of days."

"We might never see each other again."

I'd never really considered that until exactly this moment. This second here, this little interaction that's about to be interrupted by my horse, is the last bit of time I'll ever have with Levy Rider. After this summer, after all he's taught me about horses and life and love and everything in between, I'm going to have to let him go.

For the millionth time this summer, I blink back tears.

"Hey, hey," he croons as Stormy nuzzles my pocket for a carrot that isn't there. "Don't cry, Morrigan."

"How can I not?" I sniffle. "I just—I never thought someone would be able to make me forget Fitz. And you did that. You and this horse right here."

I unlink my fingers from around Levy and take a step back, breaking his hold on me to smooth down Stormy's long mane. The mare flicks her ears back and forth as she lips my elbow, trying to tell me in her horse language she knows I've got a treat hidden somewhere for her. It's in my boot, but I don't tell her. She slowly snuffles along my leg until she gets to the top of the leather and then snorts a second time.

Levy chuckles at the two of us. "You know, if I didn't know any better, I'd say you'd had this horse forever."

"A forever summer, Levy."

"What's a forever summer?" He tilts his head just a little to the left at the question.

The corner of my mouth quirks upward as I pull the carrot from my boot and watch Stormy crunch it to little orange bits. "You know," I start, not looking at him but still looking at the gray horse. "One of those summers that seem endless, hot, long days with cool summer nights under the stars. The ones where you stop counting the days of the week because they don't matter anymore. The ones where hours drag and slip and drag and slip, going by slowly and quickly all at the same time. The ones where the season makes you think anything is possible, even just for a little while."

"Was this your forever summer?"

I pause for a moment before throwing the question back. "Was it yours?"

He doesn't respond, instead giving me a quick little flash of a smile. That tells me everything I need to know.

We stand there in the quiet morning light for a little while, watching the horses while watching each other all at the same time. It's obvious he doesn't want to say goodbye because it means the end of something, while for me it signifies the beginning of my return home to Michigan. That's the thing about a forever summer. It may seem infinite, but it's not. It always comes to a crashing end.

This is our crashing end.

"So," Levy starts, rocking back and forth once from heel to toe and back again, "I guess this is it."

I bite the inside of my cheek until the skin comes off, which doesn't take much considering I've always had it as a nervous kind of habit. One hand twists around the bracelet on my arm, a small chain that doesn't hide the scars on my wrists but instead, in some way, draws attention to them. Usually I would wear a whole bunch of them at one time, but lately, just this one's been sticking with me. It doesn't feel strange anymore to cover my wrists, as if the need to do it sort of just disappeared one day with no ceremony attached to it.

"I guess so," I reply, looking down at the paperback still sitting on the grass with the cover facing up. The black horse on the cover kind of looks like one of the foals but a couple of years into the future. A little part of me feels annoyed Levy's leaving so soon, like I expected him to wait until I went back to Michigan to make his escape from Tin Star and the memory of his community service.

"I'll text you; I promise," he notes.

"I don't have a phone anymore, remember? It's part of the creek now."

"Right."

There's a pause then, an awkward one, that kind of reminds me of the drive home from church the day I fainted in the pew. We haven't had a strange silence like that in a while, and I can't help that my eyes drift over to the leftovers of the barn where Declan and Ranger are hauling out charred remains of beams and setting up a saw. The two of them work in tandem, their voices floating across the summer Alabama air and hitting my ears as barely a whisper. But despite their distance, I can tell they're half working and half watching us, knowing something's about to happen. Or maybe I'm just imagining things.

"I don't know what to say or do here, Mo," Levy finally admits, scuffing a boot against the edge of the grass where the horses haven't quite mowed it down. "I've never had to say goodbye to someone like this."

My thoughts flit to the way I was forced to say goodbye to Fitz when he was shoved into the police car, lights flashing in the darkness, but I quickly process them and push them back to where they belong. Away from me. But there's something here I don't want to go away, and that's Levy.

"I'm not going back to Michigan," I blurt, the

statement coming out of my mouth before I even have the chance to censor it. "I'm staying here."

I have no idea if that's an option or not.

Levy cocks his eyebrow at me. "What do you mean, you're not going back to Michigan? Did you already talk to your dad about this?"

"Well, no, I just—what's there for me anymore, Levy? Jessie, Fitz, all my friends, and everything I ever cared about don't exist in that place anymore. I want to stay here where things matter to me. People matter to me. This horse matters to me."

Stormy splashes her muzzle in the water trough for emphasis, soaking the side of my jeans.

"Maybe if I would have known sooner—" Levy cuts himself off. "Look, Mo. If you're here, trust me, I'll see you again. Whether you're visiting or you've moved into that bedroom of yours. I'll find a way back to Tin Star, and to you."

I can't force the tears back anymore, so I let myself start to cry, and Levy doesn't stop me.

"It's been a perfect forever summer," I choke.

"It has."

Levy squeezes my hand once before he turns and doesn't look back. Even as he makes his way down the dirt drive under the Tin Star Ranch sign, his eyes are forward on the expanse of trees across the road. I watch for a while as the black truck curves and winds down the blacktop until, eventually, it disappears. When I look to my left, Rosie has her head over the fence, staring down the double yellow line like she knows her forever summer has just ended too.

The rest of the week, barn chores just aren't the same. Declan and Ranger give me the easy tasks and leave me half the days to take Stormy for rides, even though I really don't feel like riding without Levy around. We poke around the ring for half the time, walking around the property and stomping on the flowers the other half, because crushing perennials is about all I feel like doing now that Levy isn't here. I'm not grumpy. I'm just sad. And sad in a different way than when Fitz was arrested. That was a desperate kind of sad. This is more—I don't know. Something else. I don't know the words for it.

I'm in the middle of the flower garden with Stormy, letting her pluck the leaves off some plants growing around the edge, when both my mother and Dad come out of the house and stand on the wraparound porch. For a moment I think they're going to mention something about me smooshing all the flowers with Stormy's hooves, but they just stand and watch the two of us for a moment or so before Mom speaks.

"Levy texted your father. Made it to Florida okay. He said to say hello."

"Hello, Levy," I say out into the universe, picking a bit of hay from Stormy's mane.

"He also asked," Dad says with a pause, "if you had made up your mind about staying at the ranch."

My eyes dart over to where my parents are standing, Dad's head healed except for a skinny scar across his forehead that looks a subtle shade of red. Mom's wearing her jeans and that same pair of cowboy boots she's had on for two weeks now, her yellow T-shirt offsetting the blonde in her hair. They both look concerned but also curious.

Stormy spots my father once he speaks, her ears

flickering to him as she proceeds to amble over to the porch railing. It takes me a second to spot the carrot between his fingers, but as always, it took the mare no time at all. She lifts her head, gently takes it from his hand, and munches away happily while they wait for me to respond.

"I don't know," I start, the words coming out as slow as molasses. "I mean, I told him I wasn't really sure there was a reason for me to go back to Michigan. There's a reason for me to stay here. I have Stormy. I have what's left of the ranch. I can help rebuild. I don't need that home anymore. I have this one."

Mom scratches the corner of her eye. Maybe I've hurt her a little bit with my words. But they're true, and I want to stay. On top of that, I'm still injured from Levy leaving last week, so a piece of me doesn't care, but another piece tells my mouth to keep talking.

"It's not that Michigan isn't home with you, Mom...it's just that it's more like a memory, you know? This feels like a place where I belong."

"You don't have to go back." Mom's voice is quiet. "I'm going back, but this is your life now, Morrigan. You're old enough and smart enough to make your own decisions about what you want to do. But I don't want you staying here because of a boy. I want you to be staying here because of you."

"I'm staying because of a feeling. And a dream from when I was a little kid. Oh, and a horse, of course."

"What do you think, Thomas?" Mom asks, as if she and Dad haven't already had a conversation about this in the house.

"I'd be happy to have the extra help," he says. "We

can work something out so Mo's getting a living wage for her hard work here on the ranch, and we'll just take things as they go for the year. After that, I'd personally like to see her think about some schooling, either online or in the city. It never hurts to have a second option. You just don't know where those experiences might lead in the future."

"Well," Mom notes, rubbing at her eye again, and it's only then I realize she's flicking away tears. "That settles that, then."

She's sad, but she's smiling, which tells me something about her strength as a mother. I'm also sad, but I'm smiling too, which says something about me as well.

"We're having corn and barbecued steaks for supper if you're hungry." Dad clears his throat and changes the subject before the two of us melt into tears. It's the same meal we had my first night on the ranch, and now it will be the first meal I've had my first night home. "Tell the boys to come on in. There're extras. And get that horse out of my garden."

We all share a laugh that echoes over the paddocks and disappears into the late afternoon, the sound of my happiness reflecting above it all. I get to stay at the ranch. I get to stay with Stormy. And most of all, above everything else, I get to stay whole.

Chapter 18

Another week flies by without Levy, complete with cotton-candy sunsets and bright, starry skies. It's almost as if the world doesn't know he's gone from Tin Star; life goes on, and the Earth keeps spinning. In my heart, though, everything feels like it stopped in forever summer and just stuck there.

My mother flies back to Michigan on Saturday, a warm and rainy day that creates puddles in the driveway and under the horses' feet as they splash next to the paddock gates. Declan and Ranger have finished building two run-in sheds for the animals turned out in the fields, and despite the pouring rain, they all stand out and get drenched. The rain here in Alabama feels different than the rain back in Michigan, though. There it was cold and damp, while here the ground absorbs it like a sponge, so it doesn't stay wet for all that long. Maybe this is what it's always going to be like when it rains at the end of the summer, the Alabama days creeping steadily into September.

It doesn't take long before Dad's back on his feet and out all day with the two ranch hands. In conjunction with an Alamo City construction company called Zen, the barn's looking almost better than it did before the fire. They even managed to salvage the back half of the stable, so the building has this neat two-toned look to it now. That's about all I can tell from the outside—the boys and Dad have tried to keep me out, saying it's still a little dangerous to be walking around in there.

It's all kind of an interesting reminder of the night Levy spent in my bedroom, the thunderstorm, the fire, and how everything changed—for the better, as it turns out.

A couple of days after Mom leaves, Dad shows up at the ranch with a new phone for me so I don't completely lose touch with her. I think he suspects I'll also start texting Levy on it, but though his number tickles at my fingers, I don't actually send a message until the Tuesday after.

I sit in bed for a half an hour at five in the morning, trying to craft the perfect note to break the ice. Finally, after all that time, I settle on the most basic message I can think up.

Morrigan: —Hi.—

A quarter of a minute ticks by before I see little dots bouncing at the bottom of the screen, indicating he's writing a message back.

Levy: —Good morning, sunshine. Happy birthday. About time you got a new phone.—

Morrigan: —My birthday's in October. And how'd you know it was me?—

Propping myself up on my elbow, I stuff my pillow in the crevice to keep my hand from going numb. I didn't expect a response so soon, but I suppose I should since I'm sure the horses at Amberwood don't wait for him any more than the horses at Tin Star did.

Levy: —I know, but I'm going to miss it. So I thought I'd give you something a little bit early. Plus, I don't want the horses to destroy it, so you've got to look for it now. And of course, your father gave me your number when he picked up the phone.—

Morrigan: —Now? It's half past five.—

Levy: —Meaning you're late for work. I'll give you a hint. Your gift isn't in the house.—

I snort out loud.

Morrigan: —Are you sure my gift isn't a new coffee machine? Because I think that's what Dad's going to need after this.—

Levy: —Get up, Mo. I only have half an hour before I have to be on a horse. Once you get outside, video chat me.—

Rather reluctantly, I unwrap myself from the blankets and shove my legs into the same pair of jeans I wore yesterday. Declan's got the morning feeding and watering today to give me time to sleep in, but of course, I couldn't manage to get any shut-eye past my usual alarm. That might explain why he looks so surprised to see me out of bed when I walk down the hall and he's at the coffee machine.

"Mine," I grumble, pointing to the coffee machine.

"Yours what?" Declan smiles, raising an eyebrow at my pajama top coupled with dirty pants. I've long since stopped caring what he and Ranger think of my attire because they certainly don't give a crap what I think about theirs.

"Coffee. I need it. I have to call Levy. He's put me up to some scavenger hunt."

Declan nods. "Ah, so today's the day. Good thing everything got set up a few days back. We were just waiting for you to finally text him."

"You're in on this?" I steal the cup of black coffee Declan poured out from underneath the machine. "For

174

that, you're giving up this first cup."

I take a sip of the boiling hot brew. It scalds my throat as I shove on my dusty boots and stomp outside. The morning is colder than the other days have been, the weather starting to change for the fall. My arms get goose bumps as I step into the light breeze, the bushes at the end of the porch bristling in the wind. I probably should have put on a sweater, but I can't say I'm fully awake yet. Maybe at the bottom of this cup, I'll feel a little better.

Taking another gulp, I punch the call button next to Levy's name. It rings once before he picks up, and his face is emblazoned across the shiny screen of the phone. My heart skips a beat at the sight of him, long hair tied back in a bun on his neck and his face even more tanned than I remember it being at the end of the summer. Florida looks like it agrees with him in the same way Alabama agrees with my father. I don't know exactly where he is, but it's quiet, and the light is pale.

"Well, hello. I see you didn't much bother getting dressed."

"I have pants on. That's the best anyone around here can ask for on my day off," I reply, a smile creeping over my face even though I'm trying to feign grumpiness. "Now what's this about a birthday present?"

"Well, hang on there. Can't you take me to see my favorite girl before we jump right into the present giving?"

"I thought I was your favorite girl," I joke, running a hand through my hair the moment I think about the fact I haven't brushed it yet.

"Okay, favorite girl horse, then." He flashes me a

signature grin. "How're things there anyway?"

"Same old. New barn. It's starting to really come along. They think they should be finished entirely in a couple of weeks. Zen is doing a nice job." I take a seat on the rocking swing and drink another mouthful of coffee before setting the mug on the ledge. "How's Ocala?"

"It's different. The farm is big. Horses are big. Traffic is a nightmare. You'd probably love it. It's more like Michigan."

I don't bother to ask how he knows what Michigan is like because I've never really thought about the fact that he's probably seen more of this country than I have. I suppose that's not really any great feat—I've been to exactly five states now.

"I thought you said you only had a few minutes until a ride time?" I remind him, rocking back and forth on the swing with a little squeak.

Declan comes out of the house and bangs the screen door just loud enough so I'll notice he's there. "Hello, Levy." Declan walks past with his new cup of coffee, his boots clomping down the front steps. "Rosie misses you."

Levy laughs as Declan ambles off down the driveway, gravel crunching under his feet.

"So the ride time?" I repeat the question, scratching a stray hair off my forehead.

"That was just to get you out of bed. I'm off today. I'm actually under the covers myself."

I curse a string of mild profanities, some that I learned back in Michigan and a few others Declan and Ranger have spouted while working on the barn. "Levy, that's so not fair. Can't I look for this present later?"

"Hey, you're the one who messaged me, sunshine. Plus, now you're up, so you might as well get treasure hunting in that cute pajama shirt of yours. It's familiar, but I can't remember why."

Looking down, I realize I'm wearing the band shirt I had on when I ran into Levy in the kitchen one of the first mornings on the ranch. When I mention this to him, he just grins, and after that, we're silent for a while as we watch each other think through the screens of our phones.

"I miss you," he announces, breaking the quiet like he's been holding on to the words for weeks.

My lip quivers a little bit, but I tell myself I can't cry, not now. I've cried so much for one summer I should probably not be allowed any tears until after the new year. "I miss you too, cowboy."

"Use my real name, Morrigan. Tell me you miss me for real."

I sigh, crunching myself up as small as I can go on the swing. Tell him I miss him for real? Every day I've thought about him, how he's changed me, yet he's kept me the same. The way he was gentle and kind and safe. The moment and the sentiment seem too personal for the great outdoors of the ranch, but with the sun coming up over the trees all lemon yellow like Levy's old house, perhaps the ranch is the most private space of all.

And in that private space, five words come out.

"I think I love you."

Levy raises one hand to his face to rub at his jawline before he speaks. "You think, or you know?"

"I know," I reply with quiet confidence. I do know I'm in love with him, more than I've been in love with anyone else. More than Fitz and more than Evan in ninth grade, and more than I love the way the sunset looks in the Alabama sky. The love was enough to let Levy go, let him have his life in Florida without me, and hopefully, the love is enough for him to come back when he's ready.

I swing back and forth twice, anxiously waiting for the response I can only hope is coming.

"I know too," he finally responds, as if the pause in the conversation was more for emphasis than anything else.

We both smile then, my face unable to hide the way I feel for him.

"You saved me," I whisper, almost to myself but just loud enough for him to hear.

"Stormy saved you. I just helped a little." He clears his throat again. "Now are you ready for your treasure hunt? You're already out of bed, so you're pretty much halfway to the end."

"Declan told me he and Ranger were in on the whole thing. I could just ask him where this prize is."

"They won't tell you because they don't know what it is." Levy laughs. "Come on, play along."

"Fine, what's my first clue?"

"Find black beauty."

"What?" I furrow my brow. "Black beauty? Like, wait, you mean the book?"

"My lips are sealed."

I try to think about where I left the paperback last. It was on the countertop, then in the grass when Levy dropped it, then I was reading it in the outbuilding, and then after that, I placed it down under the swing where it's sat ever since. I reach over the edge of the seat and feel for the soft cover of the well-worn story.

"Very good." He smiles, waiting.

"Now what?"

"Now what, indeed?"

"Levy, come on, it's five in the morning. You can't really expect—" I flip open the cover of the book, and a note's stuck to the front page. The writing is undeniably Levy's, the all-capital letters scrawled over a little blue Post-It Note.

"NEIGH." LOVE, STORMY

"What kind of clue is this?" I ask, knowing full well he's not going to answer. The look on his face is too amused at my sleepiness and reactions to figuring out the scavenger hunt. "Okay, okay. This one has something to do with Stormy. Somehow. I'll go see her, and maybe she'll tell me something in horse language."

"Maybe she will." He nods, as if horse language is a real thing I'll be able to understand.

I wander off the deck and across the drive to the front paddock where Stormy's out with Rosie, nibbling on the tufts of grass that are apparently greener on the other side of the fence. Even from halfway across the lawn, I spot a little blue ribbon tied to her halter with a tag fluttering from it. It wasn't there last evening when I went to say goodnight, but then again, the horses don't usually have their halters on during turn out either.

"Okay, who tied a note to the horse?" I ask, breaking into a jog. The phone bounces up and down in my hand as I run, and I'm sure the angle isn't very flattering. I don't care, though, not this time, because I know now Levy loves me.

He laughs, and it's one of the best sounds in the world. "I got Declan to do it. He's a good sport."

Looking up and over to the barn, I see Declan and Ranger both waving in my general direction.

"They've been looking forward to this all morning."

Stormy stands still as I reach over the fence and pull the ends of the tie until the note slips off. For a second time, there's a message from Levy.

TAKE ME HOME

"Take who home?" I ask, looking down at the screen.

"Stormy."

"She is at home."

He sighs. "Her inside home, Morrigan."

"But it's not ready—Dad and them haven't even let me in yet." As I speak, a lightbulb comes on in my head. They haven't been letting me in because they've been helping Levy set this all up. "Wait, did you—?"

He nods with that same sweet grin plastered all over his face. "Show her to her renovated house."

I set the phone on the railing and grab a lead line from the post, clambering under the fence to clip it to Stormy's halter. She gives me a nuzzle of my pocket but lets out a groan when she realizes there's no new-carrot smell in there. The gate gives a squeak as it opens, everything on the ranch a little squeaky since everyone's been focused on the barn. I collect the phone again as Levy complains about being forced to stare at the morning sky, while Stormy follows me out, slow and steady as ever, stealing a bite of the long grass as we walk up to the new front half of the stable. The sound her feet make on the gravel in the morning is like music.

"Take 'er on in," Ranger notes with an oversized

180

gesture of his hand, like he's presenting me with the grand prize on some television show. "See if you can find her place."

"I thought you all said—"

"We say a lot of things, Miss Westhaver. Levy made us promise we wouldn't tell." Ranger tips his hat at me before turning back to the nail he's hammering, while Declan gives me a little smile that says he knows what's going to happen next.

"Levy, did you really put them up to this? You owe them."

"I owe them a million times, Mo."

Stormy gives a little pull on her lead, as if she's trying to tell me she wants to go in and see her new stall and not wait around any longer for any other clues. I give the gray mare a soft scratch on the neck before I walk beneath the overhang and through the gap where I presume doors will be placed eventually. The inside of the aisle is bright and open, with most of the stalls still just shells without doors, but the farther along the corridor I walk, the closer I get to the old part of the barn with open windows and a gentle breeze. Stuck right in between the gap where the two buildings would be is a stall with a gold nameplate on it.

Stormy—owned and loved by Morrigan Westhaver

Behind the nameplate, just a corner tucked in, is a white envelope with nothing written on it.

"Put Stormy in her home so you can have a look at what's in the envelope," Levy encourages. His words come out soothing and gentle as I stick the phone in between the bars of the stall wall so it doesn't fall. I already have Stormy inside and turned around before he can even finish his sentence, but I keep talking as I slip the halter over her head before she dives for a pile of hay in the corner.

"What's in the envelope?" I shut the stall door and close the latch.

"Can you tip me up against the bars so I can at least watch you open it?"

I laugh, reaching over to adjust the device before plucking the envelope from behind the nameplate and ripping open the top. It feels thin, like a card, but thick enough that it's not empty or just has a clue written on the underside. This is it; this is the present, and Levy's lying there on the other end of the phone in his bed waiting for my reaction. I hope I have the right one.

Inside is a piece of cardstock. It looks blank until I flip it over. On the other side, amid bright greens and the blue of the river, is a painting of Stormy and me splashing in the creek. The hues are beautiful and run together in a kind of watercolor, shades of yellow indicating the angle of the sun while the gray of the mare's hide has perfect dapples. Little flecks of water are suspended in the air while the girl on the horse's back—me—is laughing and happy.

At the very bottom of it all, written by Levy in his blockish text, is the caption that captures everything best.

WILD HEARTS CAN'T BE BROKEN

Chapter 19

Levy doesn't come back to Alabama.

The months roll past like country hills, our conversations lapsing from twice a day to every evening before bed, and then every other day as the realities of our lives take over. Once he begins his farrier course, he's busy studying, and when the trail rides start back up again, I'm following along with them every couple of hours from dawn until dusk. My day swaps from horse to horse to horse, but my early morning rides are always reserved for Stormy so she can be the first to splash in the water with whoever is lucky enough to draw Rosie's name from the hat.

I probably could worry myself sick over Levy, but I try not to. Admittedly there have been a few lonely nights where I've thought about what exactly I'm doing waiting up for a boy who might never come back home, but then a part of me knows he has to come back. He just has to because I believe he will.

And every time I look at that painting of me and Stormy he had done God knows when, I believe it even more.

October spills into November and then through to December, the weather changing to indicate the coming of Christmastime. The rides get put on hiatus, the horses are given a seasonal break, and the rest of us take it as a partial vacation. Dad says everyone deserves to have a break, and with the two of us at the house, he tells Declan and Ranger to take time with their families and that we'll keep Tin Star under control.

Everything and nothing happens, all at once, the forever summer leaning more toward a sentiment that's forever Alabama.

The third morning of our break—the day before Christmas Eve—is cold, the sky a clear cerulean like the ocean, but the wind bitter on the edges. The trees wobble back and forth with the force of the breeze, horses' manes and tails whooshing as Dad considers whether they might need blankets this winter. I don't know enough about the topic to participate, so I just listen to him think out loud.

"I'm not even sure I could get blankets in town. I might have to go north or order them online," Dad mumbles, drinking his coffee, all wrapped up in a lumberman jacket on the porch.

"Mhmm."

"The Almanac says this winter's going to be a chilly one. We might even get snow."

The mention of snow reminds me of Michigan, but Michigan no longer reminds me of Fitz. Instead, it reminds me my mother has offered to come to visit for the holidays. With my mother's arrival over Christmas comes her famously terrible turkey dinner I'd give anything for right about now. Dad's already bought a bird from Mr. Jackson down the road and stuffed it as per Mom's instructions. She always does it too early, and the inside gets soggy, but that's the way it's always been done, and that tradition is something I understand now the importance of holding on to.

I tug a Sherpa blanket closer around me, tucking

my socked feet up against the rocking swing. "How much snow is there usually here?" I reach for my hot chocolate and blow the steam off the top.

"Couple inches on average. Nothing much. Not like back—there."

Dad's still sensitive about mentioning Michigan around me, and honestly, I think it's probably for the best. I'd much rather talk about the horses and the barn and literally anything else, and it seems as if he shares the sentiment.

"At least enough to make a little snowman on the front lawn, like old times," I note.

This makes him smile before he dips to take another sip of his drink. "Well, it's freezing out here. I'm going to go up to Lucky Tack and see if they happen to have any blankets in for the babies. If not, I'll stop at Bernard's and see if he'll let me borrow a couple of his old ones. Did you want to come for the drive?"

I think for a second, feeling cozy in my blanket and sweatpants despite the chill. "I'll stay here."

A little gust of wind whooshes out in the yard, the new skinny trees lining the edge of the barn blowing a bit. Thankfully the angle of the house is blocking the two of us from the worst of it, but if I dare to unravel myself from the living room throw, I'd be cold too.

Dad gives me a little nod before disappearing into the house with a creak of the door as I pull my phone out from under the covers.

Morrigan: —Hey, cowboy.—

I wait for the three little dots to show up to tell me he's typing, but after a few minutes, they don't come. My fingers start to turn red from the air, and I tuck everything back in under the blanket, including my hand with the hot chocolate. The steam rises up from the mug and heats my face while I sit there quietly, watching the horses nibble on the frost-covered grass of the paddocks.

My father opens the door again a moment later, his well-worn Countryman boots on his feet and the truck keys jingling in his hand. "Last chance."

"I'm good. I'll stay here. I need some quiet time in order to get your present and Mom's gift wrapped anyway." I smile, knowing how much my parents hate surprises.

"What did you get your mother, anyway?" He's probably prodding for ideas of what to pick up when he's out in Alamo City.

"No way, not telling. You're not stealing my idea again this year. You tried that when I was ten, and you're not getting away with it a second time."

My father laughs, rubbing at the stubble of his beard and shivering a little under his jacket. "All right then, my secretive girl. I'll be gone for a few hours." He turns to step down off the porch and then pauses. "Oh, I got this for you if you want something to do while I'm gone."

From the inside of his jacket, he pulls out a package covered in snowflake wrapping paper. Dad hands it over to me as I stretch my arm out from the safety of the throw. The cold air nips at the fabric of my hoodie as I take it, a book clearly nestled inside the haphazard wrapping job. Dad was never very good at those kinds of things.

"Thank you." I pick at the edge of the tape tentatively, curious about what's inside but wanting to open it alone just in case.

"I'll see you in a bit."

"Bye, Dad."

Dad hops in the truck and switches the key in the ignition, the vehicle roaring to life with the familiar sound I hear out my window almost every morning. I wait until he's disappeared down the driveway before I place my half-empty mug on the porch to open the rest of the gift, shredding and crumpling the shiny paper up on my lap before flipping the contents over—a book, I was right—to look at the cover.

Stormy, Misty's Foal by Marguerite Henry.

Seeing Stormy's name on the cover of a book makes me smile, warming up the space behind my ribs where the hot chocolate also heated. This time, though, it's a different kind of warmth, one that comes from the caring of family and the season of giving. Even though Dad's not very good at wrapping, he's very good at buying presents, and as we're both bookworms, this lately has meant he's been bringing home piles of hardbacks from the secondhand store in Jasper Hole. He's a sucker for anything with a horse on the cover, and often as we realize much too late, the cover has nothing to do with the quality of the contents.

My phone beeps from under the covers, and I set the book down on the rocking swing.

Levy: —Morning. Guess where I am?—

Morrigan: —In bed? On a horse?—

Levy: —Better than those.—

Morrigan: —What's better than being in bed or on a horse?—

There's no response, the little typing dots appearing and then disappearing into a blank screen.

Morrigan: —Levy? Now you have to tell me.

Obviously, you're doing something exciting.—

Morrigan: —Levyyyyyyy.—

Morrigan: —Fine, don't tell me. I'll just make something up.—

Morrigan: —You're on your way to the moon on a rocket built from saddles.—

Still no response.

I sigh, my breath turning into a frosty puff that hangs in the air for a moment before dissolving into nothing. Levy must really be busy with whatever it is that he's doing to leave me off on a cliff-hanger like that one. Setting the phone down on the rocking swing, I pick up the book Dad just gifted me and open the front cover.

Morrigan—
Merry Christmas.
Love,
Dad

As I flip over to the first page with a little smile on my face, through the trees comes the crunch of tires. Perhaps Dad forgot his wallet on the way to Lucky Tack again and had to turn around in one of the driveways down the road. However, as I look up from *Stormy, Misty's Foal*, I spot an equally familiar truck pulling up the gravel. My heart realizes who it is before my head does, nearly exploding in my chest at the same time I spot the very first snowflakes falling.

Throwing the blanket off, I race in my sock feet down the porch steps to meet the vehicle by the wilted flower beds. As Levy opens the truck door and steps down from the driver's seat, I wrap my arms around his neck and pull him in for a hug like it's been an eternity since we've seen each other.

In some ways, I suppose it has been.

"You were coming here," I whisper into his neck, the scent of coconut shampoo fresh on his hair, like forever summer but in the wintertime.

He grasps his fingers behind my back and pulls me close in, the fabric of his coat soft against my face. "I told you I'd be back," he murmurs, squeezing my body as close as we can get.

"But you didn't say when."

We reluctantly break apart from our closeness, my arms still around his neck but with room to breathe. As we put some space between us, the snow flies heavier, swirling around us like we're in some kind of dream. He and I look up, flakes landing in our hair and on our hands—cold, ivory dots like little winter sparkles falling from up above.

"It never snows here," he comments, tilting his head to look at me for a second time. "Guess today must be pretty special. Just like someone I know."

A red heat flushes my face, the compliment twinging in my stomach like most compliments from Levy do.

He slips his hand down my arm and lands on my wrist, looking at the space where my sleeve has pulled back from our hug. "No band?"

"I haven't been wearing anything. Just the bracelet. It reminds me love is stronger than anything else."

"I never did ask you where it came from." He toys with the gold chain so gently I can hardly feel his warm fingers on my cold skin.

"Mom bought it for me when I was in the hospital. I think she wasn't sure how to tell me she loved me, so she gave me a gift instead."

"I like it."

"Me too."

My teeth start to chatter right at that moment, and he unzips his coat, exposing a heavy plaid shirt that clings to his shoulders. Snow has started to gather by our feet, the horses playing in the background and kicking up their heels as the white powder collects on the ground. Rosie gives a loud neigh as she takes off across the paddock, running back and forth across the fence line as she seems to suddenly realize Levy's back on the ranch.

He pulls his arms from the jacket and slings it over my shoulders.

"We could just go inside, you know," I suggest, slipping my arms through the holes.

"I don't want to, not just yet."

"Why not?"

"Because," he starts, placing his hands on my arms and rubbing them up and down for warmth, "I have something I need to say, and it's too pretty outside to say it anywhere else."

I tip my head to the side. "What do you mean, you have something to say?"

He bites his lip, just a little. "Remember when you told me on video chat a few months ago that you thought you were in love with me?"

Smiling, I nod. "You didn't say it back, so I didn't bother saying it again. But I kept thinking it and thinking you had a reason for not saying it back."

A snowflake lands on his eyelashes, and it's a perfectly pointed shape until he blinks, and it melts away.

"I didn't say it back because I wanted to say it in

person. And I knew I'd get to, but I just wasn't sure when." He clears his throat, taking my hands into his as the snow creates a sort of curtain around us, the wind blowing a tunnel around our bodies. I'm warm here in his thick coat, and I'm also warm in the company of this boy who I love, undeniably and without limitations.

"I love you, Morrigan Rose Westhaver. I've liked you since the second you dropped that plate of corn on your father's floor, but I've loved you for so many more moments than that."

Levy pulls me close, running his hands through my shaggy hair before drawing me in against his lips. They're cool for a moment, then warm up as mine press against them, the smell of mint and bourbon on the air and in my mind as I kiss him back. We stay like that until the snow freezes us out, horses in the paddocks retiring to their run-in sheds as the evergreens turn white and frosty. My heart and his beat in time with one another, one pulse, one moment together in what we'll always remember as our forever summer.

A word about the author...

Nicole Bea is a short-story author and novelist who primarily focuses on contemporary teen fiction. An avid storyteller since childhood, she has honed her skills through a variety of educational programs including management, sociology, legal studies, and cultural diversity in the workplace, most recently engaging in coursework about communication for technologists. In addition to writing for young adults, Nicole is also a technical writer for a global manufacturer of CPAP masks, machines, and other products that manage sleep-disordered breathing.

When she isn't busy updating her manuscript portfolio or catching up on her To Be Read pile, Nicole can usually be found gardening, horseback riding, or pursuing her new hobby of learning to cook. She and her husband share their home in Eastern Canada with a collection of multicolored cats and a lifetime's worth of books.

~*~

Find Nicole online at:
http://www.nicolebea.com